"Haven't you heard a word I've said?" Jessica asked, pouncing on Elizabeth's chair and spinning her around.

"I've heard every word. I'm just not going to audition, that's all."

"You have got to be kidding!" Jessica wailed. "This is the opportunity of a lifetime. Soap operas don't search for blond-haired, blue-eyed identical twins every day of the week."

Elizabeth stood up and faced her sister. "Look, Jess, I know you're really excited about this, but it's just not for me. I've got more important things to do than become a star of daytime TV."

"Acting is a career, you know," Jessica retorted.

"Look, it's the same problem I had with the Miss Teen Sweet Valley competition. Beauty contests and soap operas are in the same category."

"You just haven't given them a chance," Jessica protested.

"Sorry, Jess," Elizabeth said firmly, "but there are just some things you can't talk me into."

Bantam Books in the Sweet Valley High series
Ask your bookseller for the books you have missed

SWEET VALLEY High®

SOAP
STAR

Written by
Kate William

Created by
FRANCINE PASCAL

BANTAM BOOKS
NEW YORK • TORONTO • LONDON • SYDNEY • AUCKLAND

RL 6, age 12 and up

SOAP STAR
A Bantam Book / May 1992

Sweet Valley High is a registered trademark of Francine Pascal

Conceived by Francine Pascal

Produced by Daniel Weiss Associates, Inc.
33 West 17th Street
New York, NY 10011

Cover art by James Mathewuse

ISBN 0-553-29231-5

Published simultaneously in the United States and Canada

*Bantam Books are published by Bantam Books, a division of Bantam
Doubleday Dell Publishing Group, Inc. Its trademark, consisting of
the words "Bantam Books" and the portrayal of a rooster, is Registered
in U.S. Patent and Trademark Office and in other countries. Marca
Registrada. Bantam Books, 666 Fifth Avenue, New York, New York
10103.*

PRINTED IN THE UNITED STATES OF AMERICA

OPM   0 9 8 7 6 5 4 3 2 1

One

"It's true! The rumor is really true!" Jessica Wakefield announced, sitting bolt upright on the lounge chair and holding out the latest copy of *Hollywood Digest* to her friend, Lila Fowler.

"What rumor?" Lila yawned.

Jessica wasn't about to let Lila's obvious lack of enthusiasm dampen her excitement. "Remember the other day, when I was talking about our favorite soap opera, *The Young and the Beautiful*? Remember I mentioned that they might be looking for identical twins for the show?"

Lila opened one eye and focused on Jessica. "I guess so," she mumbled.

"Well, it's right here in *Hollywood Digest*!" Jessica said, shoving the open page in front of Lila's nose. "And get this! It's not just a one-time appearance. It's for a whole week of special episodes."

Lila opened both eyes. "Really? Maybe you should audition."

Jessica could barely contain herself. "There's no maybe about it! This is a dream come true! It's perfect for me and Liz!" she said. "Listen to this. 'Natasha Talbot, the casting director for *The Young and the Beautiful*, is conducting a statewide search for a pair of identical twins. Ms. Talbot is looking for young, beautiful, charming girls who not only exude the California look but have that indefinable extra something that spells "star quality"'!"

Jessica put down the magazine and hopped out of her lounge chair. She dove into Lila's pool, swam across, did a neat flip, and swam back to where Lila sat, now reading the article.

"Those parts were made for Liz and me," Jessica said as she pushed her long hair out of her eyes. "We have the look—sun-streaked blond hair, blue-green eyes, tans. We have the style— well, at least I do, and if Liz wears my clothes, she does, too. *And* getting these parts would be a perfect excuse for buying that Jeep!"

"Whoa! Slow down, Jess," Lila said. "What does an audition for a TV show have to do with buying a Jeep?"

"Well, for one thing, the Fiat is too old and unreliable to drive into Los Angeles on a daily basis. I mean, I'm sure our parents wouldn't want us commuting to the big city in a car that might break down any second."

Lila laughed. "You have it all figured out, don't you?" she said. "I mean, it doesn't matter that *The Young and the Beautiful* is conducting this talent search statewide. It doesn't matter that you'll be up against a zillion other hopeful sets of twins. As far as you're concerned, they may as well put the names Jessica and Elizabeth Wakefield on the contracts right now."

Jessica pushed off backward and floated across the pool, hands behind her head and kicking her feet slightly. "It pays to think positively. You know that I've always wanted to be an actress. Well, this is my big chance. Just think of it, Lila! I'll get to meet Brandon Hunter, the most gorgeous man on the show."

She kicked her feet more rapidly as she fantasized about Brandon. "He'll probably develop a passionate crush on me and escort me to fabulous Hollywood parties. And while I'm decked out in a designer gown and sipping Perrier with lime, I'll meet a talent scout and be 'discovered'! Maybe Brandon will be so impressed with me that he'll ask me to co-star with him in his new movie."

Lila shook her head, then leaned over and splashed a handful of water at Jessica. "Wake up, Jessica. Those things don't happen in real life."

"Of course they do!" Jessica said, splashing Lila back. "And besides, at the very least, I'll get Brandon's autograph and the experience of a lifetime."

"*If* you and Liz get the parts."

Jessica didn't want to listen to negative comments of any kind. She figured that Lila was probably *still* jealous of the time Jessica was on the Eric Parker talk show. Well, it was really Elizabeth, *pretending* to be Jessica, who had been interviewed, but Lila didn't know that.

And then there were the interviews surrounding the Miss Teen Sweet Valley Pageant. Jessica had entered, even though Elizabeth had been totally against the entire thing. Jessica had been hooked on the glamour, but Elizabeth had protested the fact that the only thing the judges cared about was the contestants' physical appearance, not their talent or intelligence. The local media had thought the conflict between the twins was big news and had let them debate their points of view on camera.

But being on a soap opera was *different*. Acting was a profession that Jessica had had her eye on for a long time. And as far as Jessica was concerned, she and her twin sister, Elizabeth, were perfect for the parts. They were identical in every way, from their size-six figures to the dimples in their left cheeks. Even their best friends couldn't always tell them apart, particularly if they happened to dress alike and fix their hair the same way. Of course, outward appearance was where the similarity between the two girls ended. Both girls were equally popular at Sweet Valley High. Jessica was always the center of attention and the life of every party, whereas Elizabeth was down to earth and responsible.

Jessica wanted to be an actress, or some equally and spectacularly famous person. She longed for the spotlight, recognition, nonstop activity. Elizabeth's goal was to be a writer, and she was honing her talents on the school newspaper and contributing to the local newspapers on a regular basis. She had her future clearly in sight. Jessica, on the other hand, was never sure what was going to happen one minute later—and that was the way she liked it.

One thing Jessica did know: She could always count on Elizabeth in a pinch. And she was sure Elizabeth would be as thrilled as she was about the auditions.

Jessica vaulted out of the pool and grabbed her towel. "I can see it all now," she said, stretching lazily in the lounge chair. "First a guest appearance on *The Young and the Beautiful*. Did I mention, Lila, that I know every character's story line, going back four years? Then the director will like my work so much that he'll ask me to extend my contract. Then I'll land a minor role in Brandon's movie. I'll get such rave reviews that I'll have to get an agent to keep track of my schedule. By the time I graduate from high school next year, I will have made enough money to finance college and travel. . . ."

"And of course, by that time, you will have met a famous movie or rock star to date, and he'll travel wherever you travel, just to be near you," Lila added, finally getting into the spirit of things. "And he'll have dozens of eligible male friends who are just dying to meet your best pal, Lila."

"I knew you'd see the advantages of this sooner or later," Jessica said with an impish grin. "Just wait until I tell Elizabeth!"

"Maybe I should have gone swimming with Lila and Jess," Elizabeth said aloud as she sat in her room, editing the final draft of an article on budget decorating for teens. She planned to submit the finished article to *SuperTeen*, a new regional magazine based in Los Angeles.

She knew she could have taken her work with her to the pool, but with her sister and Lila around, there was no way she would have gotten anything done. Besides, this was the final draft, and if there were no mistakes on any particular page, she could turn it in as it was. Until she could afford to buy a word processor, she would have to retype any page that got water spots.

Writing was important to her. It was one thing to achieve success as a writer for Sweet Valley High's school newspaper, *The Oracle*, and for *The Sweet Valley News*, the local newspaper. But if she could sell a few of her articles to some of the regional magazines, she would be well on her way to becoming a full-fledged writer. Maybe she would even write for the *Los Angeles Times* one day. It was only a matter of time, she told herself. She would have to climb the ladder slowly.

Suddenly the door to her room flew open. The papers on her desk scattered in all directions.

"Jessica!" Elizabeth admonished. "I'm trying to work here."

"Sorry," Jessica said, bending down to help Elizabeth pick up the pages of her article. "But I have great news! It couldn't wait!"

"It never can," Elizabeth said with an indulgent grin. "What is it this time? A new guy? Poor Sam!"

"This has nothing to do with Sam," Jessica said,

sitting down on Elizabeth's neatly made bed. "I'm still as much in love with him as ever."

"I'm sure he'll be glad to know that," Elizabeth teased. She raised one eyebrow as she watched Jessica bounce on the bed, obviously eager to spill her news. Jessica had a way of turning every little thing into a major event. It was one of her most endearing, and most aggravating, qualities.

Elizabeth stacked her papers and sat back in the chair waiting for the explosion. It wasn't long in coming.

"We're going to be TV stars!" Jessica blurted out.

Elizabeth rolled her eyes. "What gives you *that* idea?"

"Look at this," Jessica said, handing Elizabeth the copy of *Hollywood Digest*, bent back to reveal the article. "It says here that *The Young and the Beautiful*, my all-time favorite soap opera, with the best actors in all of daytime TV, really is looking for a set of identical twins to play guest spots on the show for one week. Isn't that exciting?"

"I seem to remember you talking about this at Guido's the other night. And *if* we got the parts," Elizabeth said, quoting Jessica, " 'a Jeep would be the coolest way to travel.' It's all coming back to me now."

"Well, you have to admit, this is the *best* career opportunity that's come along in ages. You know I've always wanted to be an actress. Well, this is my chance. And think about how much money we could make! Mom and Dad would love it. We could even help buy the Jeep! I saw this absolutely gorgeous black Wrangler with purple trim on the Jeep lot yesterday."

"Does the article actually say anything about money?" Elizabeth asked.

Jessica scanned the fine print. "Yes, right here, it says that the twins chosen will be paid a cash stipend."

"That might be only ten dollars," Elizabeth commented.

"I'm sure it would be more than that. Anyway, just think how impressed everyone will be when we land these roles. We'll have the scoop on everyone in Hollywood—especially Brandon Hunter, the biggest hunk in show business!"

Elizabeth shook her head and laughed. "You're rambling."

"I can't help it. I'm excited. I don't think I've ever been more excited about anything in my whole life!"

"That's debatable," Elizabeth noted with a grin. "Remember the beauty contest? You were totally set on becoming Miss Teen Sweet Valley. You thought you were going to receive tons of money and fabulous prizes. And you know how *that* turned out!"

Jessica laid back on the bed and kicked her feet up into the air. Then she swung them down and leaped onto the floor. "Miss Teen Sweet Valley was nothing compared to this! This is *real life!*" she declared. "What do you say, Liz? Let's go for it!"

"I can't do it," Elizabeth said. She turned back to her papers.

"Haven't you heard a word I've said?" Jessica

asked, pouncing on Elizabeth's chair and spinning her around.

"I've heard every word. I'm just not going to audition, that's all."

"You have to be kidding!" Jessica wailed. "This is the opportunity of a lifetime. They don't search for blond-haired, blue-eyed identical twins every day of the week."

Elizabeth stood up and faced her sister. "Look, Jess, I know you're really excited about this, but it's just not for me. I've got more important things to do than become a star of daytime TV," she said.

Jessica's hands jammed onto her hips. "Like what?"

"I want to spend more time with Todd, for one thing," Elizabeth said. "I mean, we practically *just* got back together after that awful Kris Lynch episode. The last thing I want to do is spend what little free time I have away from Todd. Besides, I'm trying to use every bit of my spare time to submit articles to regional magazines. I'm working on my career here, Jess."

"So am I," Jessica retorted. "Acting is a career, you know. And speaking of Kris Lynch . . . don't forget *I* helped you out with that problem. I think you owe me a favor. If it hadn't been for me, your relationship with Todd and your friendship with Enid, not to mention your reputation, might have been permanently shredded."

"I realize that. If you hadn't found out that Kris had read my journal and that he was spreading nasty rumors all over school, I don't know what would have happened," Elizabeth said honestly.

"And don't forget that I told Todd and Enid the truth so that they wouldn't think that *you* were the one telling all their precious secrets to the kids at school. They apologized because of *my* great sleuthing abilities."

"I appreciate everything you did," Elizabeth said. "But it goes against my principles to audition for a soap opera. It's the same problem that I had with the Miss Teen Sweet Valley competition. Beauty contests and soap operas are in the same category—looks are the most important thing, not substance, not intelligence, not reason. As a matter of fact, I can't stand *The Young and the Beautiful*! The few times I've been around when you've been glued to the set have been enough to turn me off soaps forever."

"You just haven't given it a chance. If you'd watch it long enough to get into the characters and their story lines, you'd understand the attraction it has for millions of viewers nationwide."

"Well, I just don't understand why anyone would want to waste their time watching brainless girls with their equally brainless boyfriends act their way through sickeningly sweet and completely unbelievable plots! The actors must all go to the same dentist, because they all have the same dazzling smiles. I don't think it even matters if they can act, just as long as their teeth look good on camera."

"How can you say they can't act?" Jessica countered. "It takes a lot of work to memorize lines on a daily basis. Take Brandon Hunter, for instance. He may be gorgeous, but he's a truly great actor. I cried when he broke up with his girlfriend, Melody, on the show. He was so hurt, so vulnerable. And she was such a witch!"

Elizabeth threw up her hands. "You're impossibly addicted. About the only thing I'd cast Brandon Hunter as is a tree—they're both equally wooden. I tell you, Jess, if I were a writer on one of those shows, I'd show those actors a meaty plot!"

"So you'll do it?" Jessica asked hopefully.

"No!" Elizabeth said, rolling her eyes again at Jessica's backward attempt at logic. "Sorry, Jess," she added firmly, "but there are just some things you can't talk me into."

Two

Jessica didn't mention the soap opera auditions again until dinner that night. But as soon as Mrs. Wakefield set the chicken and zucchini casserole on the table, she plunged right in with her news.

"Guess what?" Jessica said. "I found this really great opportunity for Liz and I to help pay for that Jeep Wrangler we've been talking about."

"What's that?" Mr. Wakefield asked. "Jeeps cost a *lot* of money."

"This would pay quite a bit of money," Jessica went on as Elizabeth concentrated on her plate. "I saw an advertisement in *Hollywood Digest*. The producers of *The Young and the Beautiful* are looking for identical twins to appear on the show for a week. I thought it would be a good idea for Elizabeth and me to try out."

"What do you think, Liz?" her father asked.

"This is more Jessica's idea than mine," Elizabeth said. "She's the one who wants to be an actress. I'm not really that thrilled about soap operas. Besides, I'm pretty busy right now."

"C'mon, Liz," Jessica cajoled. "A week! That's all I'm asking for. A week's work that might make us a lot of money. Look. We need a new car. The Fiat is on its last legs. It breaks down about every five minutes. And what about that word processor you've been wanting?"

"Somehow I doubt that a week's work on a soap opera will pay you enough to buy a Jeep *and* a computer," Mrs. Wakefield replied. "But it might help. Where is the show filmed?"

"Not far away," Jessica said. "In Los Angeles. Just think of the experience we would have! And all the people we would meet," she added enthusiastically. "I can't believe that Liz would turn something like this down just because she's *busy*."

"We probably wouldn't even get the parts," Elizabeth said, smiling in spite of herself. "You talk as if the decision had already been made."

"But that's just the point," Jessica reasoned. "We could at least try out. Who knows? Maybe we'd get lucky."

"It sounds as if you two need to discuss this further," Mr. Wakefield said. "I don't really see a problem in the girls trying out or performing on a show like that for a week. Do you, Alice?"

"I'm sure it would be fine, and Los Angeles isn't too far away—" Mrs. Wakefield began.

"See, Liz!" Jessica exclaimed. "It's OK with Mom and Dad!"

"I told you that it was against my principles," Elizabeth argued. "I think soap operas are all fluff

13

and no substance, and I wouldn't be caught dead on one! Mom, Dad? Don't you see my point?"

Mrs. Wakefield laughed. "We said it was OK. But we're not siding with either one of you. If you want Elizabeth to do this with you, then the convincing will have to come from you, Jessica. And Elizabeth, if you don't want to do this, no one is going to force you. We're just the neutral third party."

Mr. Wakefield took a bite of his casserole and smiled. "Neutral! It reminds me of that beauty contest awhile back!" he exclaimed. "For once, I'd like to see something neutral in this house!"

"I've just about had it with Jessica trying to convince me to try out for that stupid soap opera," Elizabeth told her best friend, Enid Rollins, on the phone the next evening. "She's spent every spare minute of the past twenty-four hours coming up with reasons why I should change my mind."

"Shades of Miss Teen Sweet Valley," Enid said. "What are you going to do?"

"I'm *not* going to audition. Actually, the whole thing is pretty funny. And I guess it's all right to have Jessica badgering me every ten minutes. If she stopped, I'd begin to wonder what devious plan she was hatching to catch me completely off guard."

"Yeah, that sounds like Jessica. Hey, are you still going to Amy Sutton's party tonight?" Enid asked. "Hugh and I will be there," she added. Enid had recently gotten back together with her boyfriend, Hugh Grayson. Elizabeth couldn't wait to see them at the party. It was so much fun watching them act like lovebirds and knowing that she had been a big part of their reunion.

Elizabeth switched the phone to her other ear and put on an earring. "Of course I'm going to the party. In fact, I'm looking forward to it because maybe Jessica will find something to take her mind off *The Young and the Beautiful*. Truth is, I'm getting tired of finding new ways to say no."

"And Jessica can be pretty persistent," Enid commented wisely.

"Well, listen, I'd better finish getting ready," Elizabeth said. "See you at the party."

"OK," Enid said. "We'll see you there."

Jessica came into her room just as Elizabeth had finished dressing. As usual, the contrast between Elizabeth and her sister was startling. Elizabeth was wearing her new ocean-blue blouse and a pair of darker blue denim jeans. Jessica had on a tight, fluorescent green miniskirt and a matching top. Over the top she wore a sheer, shimmery, chiffon-print blouse that was tied in a knot at her waist. Her earrings dangled to her shoulders and picked up the multitude of colors in her blouse.

"You look really nice," Jessica said.

"So do you," Elizabeth replied. Then she waited, instinctively knowing that more was coming.

"That blue blouse brings out the color of your eyes perfectly," Jessica continued.

Elizabeth stifled a chuckle. Just last week, Jessica had told her that the same blouse made her look like an old-fashioned schoolmarm.

"I'll bet your eyes would absolutely shine on

camera," Jessica added innocently. "You know, some actresses with blue eyes have to wear colored contacts to make them show up on camera."

Elizabeth looked at her watch. It hadn't even been ten minutes, and Jessica was already at it again. She laughed and ignored Jessica's compliments. "And I wouldn't have to, I suppose?" she asked.

"Nope. Your eyes are perfect just the way they are," Jessica said.

"Look! Sam's here!" Elizabeth announced as she peeked out her window and saw his car. "We don't want to be late for Amy's party."

Jessica ran down the stairs to meet Sam, temporarily diverted from her campaign. As Elizabeth followed her, she determined to keep the conversation on the way to the party on topics *other* than acting.

"Do you have a race this weekend, Sam?" Elizabeth asked as she climbed into the back seat of Sam's car. She was riding to Amy's party with Jessica and Sam because Todd and his father were building flower boxes for their backyard. He had told her that he would meet her at the party later.

"Saturday morning," Sam said, obviously pleased that Elizabeth was interested. Jessica had made it clear long ago that watching him dirt-bike race was not her favorite pastime. He drove down Calico Drive and turned right at the intersection. "I have to leave the party a little early tonight because I have to get up at five o'clock to drive up the coast to the track in Santa Barbara."

"Santa Barbara?" Jessica asked. "You didn't tell me you were going to Santa Barbara! There are

16

tons of cute little antique shops and clothing stores down near the beach there. I hope you're taking me with you."

"I'd love to have you go," Sam said, smiling. "You can cheer me on, and then we'll hit the town afterward. How does that sound?"

"Great!" Jessica said, laying her hand across the back of the seat so that it touched Sam's neck.

"Hey, Liz," Sam said. "Would you and Todd like to come along?"

"Thanks, but I have a lot of homework and writing to catch up on this weekend," Elizabeth told him. "And Todd and I made plans for a picnic on the beach and maybe a little bodysurfing." What she didn't say was that she would be happy to have a day away from her twin's haranguing. If she heard one more word about *The Young and the Beautiful* or Jessica's missed chance to meet Brandon-the-Hunk, she thought she might scream.

The party was in full swing by the time they arrived. Amy's boyfriend, Barry Rork, was passing out sodas to Bruce Patman, Neil Freemount, Tom McKay, and Ken Matthews. Neil's girlfriend, Penny Ayala, and Ken's girlfriend, Terri Adams, were standing behind the couch, munching on chips and discussing the details of the latest Sweet Valley Gladiators football practice. Ken was the star quarterback, Terri was the team's assistant manager, and Penny was the editor-in-chief of *The Oracle*.

Elizabeth was also glad to see Enid and Hugh in the crowd.

Lila greeted them as they entered the living room. "Hi!" she said. "Come join the crowd!"

"Hi, everybody," Jessica called to the whole room. "I hope you haven't started without me!" She stopped in front of Lila and twirled around, displaying her new outfit. "Do I look like Hollywood, or what?" she asked.

"Getting ready for your new starring role, I see," Lila replied with a smile.

"It pays to be prepared," Jessica said, sitting on the couch and scooting over to make a place for Sam.

Sam sat down next to Jessica and put his arm around her. There was more room on the sofa, but Elizabeth held back from sitting for a moment, secretly smiling at the way Jessica assumed that no party really started until she got there. *She probably would be a good actress*, Elizabeth thought.

"Speaking of Hollywood—" Lila began, looking directly at Elizabeth.

Uh, oh, Elizabeth thought. *Here it comes!*

"Hi, twins, Sam," Winston Egbert said, interrupting Lila as he strolled over to the group with his girlfriend, Maria Santelli. Winston was Sweet Valley High's class clown, but also a sweet, down-to-earth guy. Maria, a member of the cheerleading squad, was the daughter of Sweet Valley's mayor. Both were Elizabeth's good friends, and she was glad to have a couple of allies besides Enid and Hugh around, since she could tell where Lila's comment was about to lead.

"Hey, Liz," Winston said, winking at her. "What's this I hear about you two becoming soap stars?"

Elizabeth rolled her eyes.

Jessica cut off Winston's chuckle with a quick

18

wave of her hand. "Listen to this," she said, looking around at the group. "Liz and I have this wonderful opportunity to try out for parts on *The Young and the Beautiful.* The show is looking for identical twins, and if we're chosen, we'll get to appear on a week's worth of episodes."

"It's about time someone did something exciting around here," Bruce remarked. "Sweet Valley is about as dull as you can get."

"Oh, I don't know," Enid said. "I think Sweet Valley's been pretty exciting lately. I mean, we've had talk show hosts come to town, a beauty pageant, police chases, and then there was last season's wild and crazy football championship."

"That's right," Elizabeth added with a smile. "Besides, a week of TV appearances would hardly make us stars. Jess thinks we would suddenly be rich and famous and invited to all the biggest Hollywood parties."

"*And* get that Jeep we both want," Jessica put in. "We *would* make a lot of money," she added, "and we'd get the inside scoop on a real television studio. I can't imagine why Elizabeth won't agree to audition."

Several pairs of curious eyes turned toward Elizabeth, and at that moment she could have cheerfully strangled her mirror-image sister.

"Are you scared?" Bruce teased.

"Hardly," Elizabeth told him good-naturedly. "I'm just not interested in being on a soap opera. I have no desire to watch them. Why should I audition to *be* on one?"

"For the experience," Amy said.

"It would be something to write about in your

newspaper column," Terri mentioned. "I'd be very interested in reading about how those shows are put together. It must take a million people!"

"That's the researcher in her," Ken said fondly. "She wants to know the ins and outs of everything."

"Well, I know why *I'd* audition," Lila said. "To meet famous men! *I'd* try out with Jessica for sure, if we could pass for twins."

"So really, Liz," Penny asked. "Why *don't* you want to try out for the show?"

Everyone's attention was suddenly back on Elizabeth. She knew she had to say something.

"It's just that I don't want *this* particular experience, and I don't particularly want to meet famous men," Elizabeth insisted, looking directly at Jessica. "I already *have* a pretty famous basketball star as my boyfriend!"

Everyone laughed. "She's got you there, Jess," Lila said.

"How about for the money?" Neil asked.

"We don't even know how much money is involved," Elizabeth countered. "The article didn't actually name a sum."

"But you know how much some of these soap stars get paid," Jessica remarked. "Thousands of dollars for only a little bit of work!"

"You're dreaming, Jess," Elizabeth told her. "I can't imagine that two amateurs would get paid very much. Certainly not enough to buy a Jeep *and* a computer."

"But you have to admit that a few thousand dollars would go a long way toward a down payment on at least one of those," Jessica argued playfully.

"Well, maybe so," Elizabeth admitted.

"If not for the money, how about the glamour?" Barry added.

"Hey, give me a break!" Elizabeth said. She put her hands up in mock self-defense. "Did Jessica call you all before the party and set this up?"

Suddenly, in the background, Elizabeth heard the doorbell. "That must be Todd," she said quickly. "I'll be happy to answer it for you, Amy." She hurried away before anyone else stood up.

Elizabeth opened the door and was glad that it was indeed Todd. She immediately threw her arms around him.

"Wow! What's all this?" Todd asked after he had hugged and kissed her hello.

"I'm glad you're here," Elizabeth said with a laugh. "Jessica won't give up on this soap opera thing, and now she has everyone at Sweet Valley High trying to persuade me, too."

"Come on. Let's get something to drink and go out on the patio," Todd suggested. "I've missed you since school let out."

Elizabeth leaned her head against his shoulder. She had never been so happy to see him. She thought his tall, lean, muscular build was perfect. Best of all, she knew she could always count on Todd to understand her feelings.

Sure, they had split up a few times—once when Todd and his family had moved to Vermont, and more recently, when the twins' older brother, Steven, had almost eloped and Todd had panicked a little. He had decided that he and Elizabeth were becoming too set in their ways and had suggested a trial separation.

But Todd had finally realized that he and Elizabeth weren't together just because it was convenient or comfortable. They were together by choice, because they loved each other. The many ups and downs in their relationship had only served to strengthen their love. Neither cared that Jessica always teased them about acting like a boring old married couple.

Elizabeth smiled contentedly as she snuggled closer to Todd. She liked the secure and stable feeling she got with him. She liked knowing that they were there for each other.

Like now.

Elizabeth and Todd each poured a cup of juice and headed for the patio. They took seats on a stone bench that overlooked the Suttons' terraced herb garden.

Todd set his glass on a low table and put his arm around Elizabeth. "Now tell me what's going on," he said.

Elizabeth grinned. "Oh, it's the same old thing. Jessica's got her mind set on something, and it's the only thing she can think about. Remember, I told you over the phone last night about her idea for us to audition for *The Young and the Beautiful*. Well, ever since then, she hasn't let up."

"What has she done?"

"What *hasn't* she done!" Elizabeth said, shaking her head. "She's tried every ploy she can think of. She's tried guilt—you know, moaning and sighing aloud when she knows I can hear her, complaining how I'm damaging any chance she has of a career in acting. She's tried the sympathy appeal—reminding me of how she's saved me from a scrape or two, and how it's only fair that I return the favor."

"Well, she *has* helped you out in a couple of pinches. She did get us back together and straighten out that whole mess with Kris. I'll always be grateful to her for that," Todd remarked, ruffling Elizabeth's hair.

"But then, you've done the same for her," Todd continued. "Look at how you saved her from running away with that Good Friends cult, and how you helped her win the beauty pageant. Even though you were so strongly opposed to the contest, you stood in for Jessica during the bathing suit competition instead of letting her lose. I'd say you're about even."

"Not according to Jessica," Elizabeth told him. "Last night she 'accidentally' left an article about actresses' salaries open on my desk next to an ad for the word processor that I'm saving for."

"That was clever, all right," Todd agreed.

"And she's been talking it up in front of Mom and Dad at dinner, emphasizing how far a fat paycheck could go toward buying that Jeep she has her heart set on. I'm not even sure how much money really is involved. I certainly don't think it's as much as Jessica is counting on. She thought the prize for the winner of the beauty pageant was going to be ten thousand dollars, and it ended up being only a hundred!"

"That *was* quite a difference." Todd smiled. "You have to admit, though, Jessica *would* be a good actress. She knows how to work a crowd. She has your parents and all our friends excited."

"I don't know. Maybe I'm crazy to refuse. But honestly, I think if one more person asks me why I don't want to be a soap queen, I'll scream."

"Come on." Todd took her hand and gave it a little tug. "Why don't we grab Hugh and Enid and get out of here? I'll take you all over to my house and show you the flower boxes my dad and I built. Then maybe we could go to Dairi Burger, where all the local 'celebrities' go for a milk shake."

"Sounds good."

"And if nobody minds, we could stop by the nursery and pick up some marigolds," Todd remarked. "My mother will be happy to see the boxes filled right away."

"We'd better hurry then," Elizabeth said, checking her watch. "The nursery closes in an hour. Let's go!"

Jessica let the curtain on Amy's living-room window drop as Elizabeth and Todd drove off in Todd's black BMW, with Enid and Hugh following close behind.

"I'm beginning to think this is hopeless," Jessica said as Lila came up next to her.

"That doesn't sound like the Jessica Wakefield I know," Lila replied. "Maybe you're not trying hard enough."

Jessica sat down in the wing-back chair next to the window. "I've done everything I can think of.

None of my usual methods are working. At this rate, I'll never get on TV."

Lila flopped down in a matching chair. "Must I remind you once again that you *have* been on TV before? Not only when you were interviewed on Eric Parker's talk show," she said, "but when you and Liz helped catch the drug ring because of that picture Liz took with Regina Morrow's camera. And how about the interview before the Miss Teen Sweet Valley pageant? Your face has been all over the news."

"But this is different. This is *acting*! Being on the news or a talk show didn't make me a star. Making a guest appearance on *The Young and the Beautiful* might."

"I guess we just have to come up with a plan," Lila remarked. "Something Liz won't expect."

The two girls were quiet for a few moments. Suddenly Lila shook Jessica's arm. "I've got it!" she cried. "You have to quit bugging her. Just drop the whole subject."

"What?" Jessica shouted. "I've *got* to keep the pressure on, to wear her down!"

"That's just what you have to *stop* doing," Lila said wisely. "Liz is holding up against your pressures. What you need to do is play it cool, act as if you've given up. Then do something really sneaky, and make it look like it came from someone else."

"What do you have in mind?" Jessica leaned forward, intrigued.

Lila flipped her long hair over her shoulder and pulled her chair closer. She whispered,

"What does Liz like to do more than anything else?"

"Write and study," Jessica answered automatically.

"That's right. She really likes to research stuff and find out about things in depth. What if you sent her a letter from a fake research company, and it asked her to come to a market research discussion group for identical twins?"

"She couldn't resist that," Jessica said, warming quickly to the idea. "She'd probably want to write an article about it for one of her newspapers."

"Exactly. Then you take her to the audition instead of the research group," Lila explained. "Isn't that devious?"

"Devious, but perfect," Jessica said. "Especially since, knowing Liz, she'll go along with it once we're there. She won't let me down. She wouldn't walk out and embarrass me in front of an entire group of people."

"That's right. Liz hates to create a scene," Lila added. "She'll give in gracefully, as only Liz can."

Jessica rubbed her hands together. She stood up and smiled at Lila. Lila was her best friend—and sometimes her worst enemy—but she *always* had great ideas.

"I think we've done it," Jessica said, already envisioning their success. "Hollywood, here I come!"

Three

After the party, Jessica went to Lila's house to spend the night. The two girls stayed up until the wee hours of the morning, composing exactly the right letter. By the time they were finished, they had created a company name, a fancy letterhead on Lila's father's computer, and two very businesslike paragraphs. The letter was sure to convince Elizabeth that the research group they had invented was legitimate.

They mailed the letter on Saturday morning, before Jessica had to meet Sam to drive to Santa Barbara for his race. For the rest of the weekend, Jessica avoided mentioning auditions and soap operas in general. By Monday, Elizabeth was speaking to her sister again without a guarded expression on her face.

"What are you doing after school today?" Jessica asked casually at lunch on Monday.

"I'm stopping by the darkroom to develop some

27

pictures for an article on Sweet Valley's extracurricular activities, and then I'm dropping off the story I finished yesterday at *The Oracle* office," Elizabeth said. "Why?"

"I was just wondering if I was going to have a car to get home in since I have to stay after school for cheerleading practice," Jessica replied.

"No problem. I'll come over to the field after I'm finished, and we can drive home together."

"You know, Liz, our schedules are so complicated lately, we *really* could use that Jeep," Jessica said with just the right note of resignation in her voice. "Not as a replacement for the Fiat, but as an *extra* set of wheels."

Elizabeth nodded and slung her backpack over her shoulder. "I'm beginning to think you're right. I don't think Mom and Dad would pay for the insurance on two cars, though. We'd be better off having one car that's totally reliable. Remember what happened to Enid when she was on her way to see Hugh a few weeks ago? They missed their date, and *almost* missed getting back together—all because of that car!"

"Yeah. The Fiat has left us stranded *too many times* lately," Jessica said. "I hope we make it home today. Yesterday it broke down again when Lila and I were coming back from the mall."

"What happened? You didn't say anything or call. I was home all afternoon."

"It happens so often lately it wasn't worth mentioning. I waited until the engine cooled down, jiggled a few wires, gave the tires a swift kick, and it all started up again. But it's definitely time for a new car," Jessica said solemnly.

"Let's talk it over seriously with Mom and Dad tonight," Elizabeth suggested. "At least maybe we could go out and look at a few Jeeps and compare prices."

That was *exactly* what Jessica wanted to hear. With both of them united in their quest for a Jeep, their parents were bound to be convinced.

Jessica flew through cheerleading practice with more than her usual spark. She was closer now than ever before to getting a new vehicle—*and* there would be a very interesting letter waiting for Elizabeth when they got home.

Two hours later, the twins opened the door to their split-level house on Calico Drive, only to be hit with a blast of music coming from the living room.

"Steven must be home from college," Jessica said, momentarily forgetting to check the mail in the front hall as she ran to greet him.

"Hey, Jess, Liz," Steven called from the kitchen as the twins headed for the living room, "I'm in here."

"What are you doing home?" Jessica asked. "On a Monday yet?"

"Thanks for the sisterly welcome," Steven said with a laugh. "I finished a big exam this morning, and I don't have any more classes until Wednesday. I thought I'd come home and do my laundry."

"And down a few home-cooked meals," Elizabeth said fondly.

"Can't argue with that," Steven said. "What's new with you two?"

Elizabeth looked at Jessica and smiled. "I'll go

29

check the mail," she said, heading back out to the hallway.

"There's a chance we might audition for parts on a soap opera," Jessica whispered, "but Liz doesn't want to."

"I take it you have a plan up your sleeve," Steven commented.

"Who, me?" Jessica feigned innocence. "Nope, I've given up."

Jessica was sure that Elizabeth had heard her last words as she came back into the kitchen and dropped the mail on the table.

"Anything for me?" Jessica asked, bounding over to the table and shuffling through the stack.

"No, but there's this official-looking envelope addressed to both of us."

"What is it? A sweepstakes?" Jessica asked.

Elizabeth shrugged and tore the flap open. "It's from California Research Associates, Incorporated," Elizabeth told her. She unfolded the inner letter as Jessica inconspicuously held her breath.

"Well, read it aloud," Jessica finally said.

"OK." Elizabeth cleared her throat and began to read. " 'Congratulations, you have been chosen to participate in a unique discussion group. Our marketing research company has been asked to conduct information-gathering sessions all over California, specifically targeting the likes and dislikes of identical twins. We would be pleased if the Wakefield twins would participate. The discussion group will be held in Los Angeles on Friday . . .' et cetera. They want us to reply by phone to let them know if we can come," Elizabeth said.

"That's this Friday!" Jessica said, pretending surprise. "That doesn't give us much time. They should have given us more notice. I mean after all, it's a school day and all."

Elizabeth reread the letter, then looked up. "I don't know, Jess. It could be interesting," she said finally. "They're offering to pay our travel expenses plus fifty dollars apiece to participate."

"Really?" Jessica said, leaning over to take a look at the letter. "Well, I can always use fifty dollars. But I don't know," she said hesitantly. "Sam and I were going to go out on Friday night."

"Oh, come on, Jess. It will be a good experience," Elizabeth insisted. "I'm sure we could get special permission to get out of school a bit early on Friday. And we'll get to visit L.A. We haven't been there in a while."

Out of the corner of her eye Jessica could see Steven munching thoughtfully on an apple. *He knows*, she thought. *He knows it's a scam, but he won't say anything.*

"Why should I do this with you?" Jessica asked. "You wouldn't try out for *The Young and the Beautiful*, and that would pay a lot more than fifty dollars if we got the parts."

"Oh, c'mon, Jess. This is something totally different," Elizabeth countered. "Something reasonable. Something that doesn't compromise your principles or mine. I might even be able to write an article about it for *The Sweet Valley News*."

Elizabeth was so predictable. It was all Jessica could do not to laugh. Especially when Steven took Elizabeth's side to persuade her.

31

"Once in a while, you *could* do something that isn't wild and crazy, Jess," Steven said. "And just think. Mom and Dad would consider taking this job as very responsible—a way to help pay for the *Jeep*."

"OK, OK," Jessica said, pretending to finally concede. *Lila's plan couldn't have worked more perfectly*, she thought. "Are you sure you won't consider a trade?" she added. "I go to the discussion group for you, you go to the audition for me?"

"Not a chance," Elizabeth said with a laugh. "You know," she added, "maybe, if the article about this discussion group is good enough, I could submit it to the *Los Angeles Times*. I've always wanted to be published in the *Times*. . . ." Her voice trailed off as she headed up to her room, the letter still in her hand.

"California Research Associates, Inc.?" Steven remarked as soon as she was out of earshot. "Pretty good, Jess. But, don't you think you're being a little *too* sneaky—"

"Shh! You realize that I had no choice," Jessica said melodramatically. "This is my whole future we're talking about here."

Steven raised an eyebrow. "I don't know what you're worried about, little sister. You're already quite an actress."

"I don't know, Todd," Elizabeth said as they sipped chocolate shakes at the Dairi Burger after school on Thursday. "I'm beginning to feel guilty."

"About what? Standing up for your principles?

Is Jessica still trying to talk you into going to that audition?"

Elizabeth took a long, contemplative sip. "No. She hasn't said a word. I heard her tell Steven that she's given up."

"That's probably Jessica's way of trying to make you give in. Arguments didn't work, so now she's trying creative guilt-building. Remember the routine she pulled on you during the Miss Teen Sweet Valley Pageant? She had you convinced that you were being the least supportive twin in the history of the world."

Elizabeth giggled. "I know what she's trying to do, and it's working. And she *has* done a lot for me lately. She even helped get us back together." Elizabeth laid her hand on top of Todd's on the table. "If not for her, we might still be stuck in one giant misunderstanding. Now she's going to the twins research group with me, even though I know she doesn't really want to. What do you think?" Elizabeth asked.

Todd chuckled. "It wouldn't matter to me one way or the other. In fact, it might be kind of cool to see my girlfriend on TV. But I'll stand behind you, whatever you decide."

"I just feel as if maybe I *should* do this for her. She seems to want it so much." Elizabeth grinned and struck a dramatic pose with one hand behind her head, her chin held high in the air. "Who knows? Maybe I could bring new depth to a shallow profession!"

"Hold that pose!" Todd aimed and clicked an imaginary camera. "It sounds as if you've made up your mind to go to the audition."

"I haven't completely decided. I don't even know when it is. I think I'll tell her after the twins discussion group tomorrow that I'll do it. After all, it's only an audition. We probably won't even get the parts. Then I won't have anything to worry about, will I?"

Four

"Ready to go, Liz?" Jessica asked, bounding up to her during lunchtime on Friday. "I turned in the note from Mom, and it's all set with the office for us to leave early."

"I need to do one more thing at *The Oracle* office, but we should have plenty of time to get to Los Angeles if we leave right after that."

Jessica's smile wavered as she looked at her sister's peach chinos and matching big shirt with its floral appliqué on the pocket. "But I was hoping we'd have time to go home and change. Put something flashy on—you know, to make a good impression."

Elizabeth looked down at her outfit. "What I'm wearing should be fine. After all, it's just going to be a bunch of people sitting around a room and talking about what it's like to be a twin."

Jessica twirled around. "Don't you think it would be nice if we looked *alike*?" she coaxed as

35

they walked along the hallway toward *The Oracle* office. "Besides, we should look our best, because of—uh . . . because you should take your camera, and maybe we can have someone take a picture of us for you to submit with your article," she added quickly.

Elizabeth checked her hair as they passed the glass display case that had just been hung outside *The Oracle* office.

"You're probably right. My hair needs combing, and my makeup could use a touch-up." Her eyes twinkled as she sped down the hallway with Jessica close behind. "I'll hurry, OK?"

"That's the spirit," Jessica said, following her through the door of the office with a little skip. "Just get what you need, and let's go!"

A few minutes later, they were out the door and practically jogging to the car.

"Hey! Slow down, Jess!" Elizabeth said as she lugged her heavy backpack, her camera, and the layouts for the spread on student activities that she was working on for next week's issue.

"I just don't want us to be late, that's all," Jessica said. She opened the door for Elizabeth and helped her stow her stuff in the trunk.

"You're awfully excited about this discussion group," Elizabeth commented, glancing sideways at her twin as she started the car.

Is Elizabeth beginning to suspect something? Jessica worried silently. She had to be more careful—at least until they got to L.A. Maybe she should tell her the truth now? No, that would be the worst thing she could do. It might ruin everything. Jessica hesitated only a second, then had the perfect

36

answer. "I already know what I'm going to spend my fifty dollars on," she quipped. "I saw this great sweater at the mall."

"Figures," Elizabeth said, laughing. "So much for saving money toward the Jeep."

"That, too," Jessica told her. "I'll save part and spend part. Saving for a rainy day is one thing, but depriving yourself along the way won't make the rainy day much fun."

"May I quote you on that?"

"Of course."

Twenty minutes later, they were well on their way to Los Angeles. It didn't seem long at all before they were entering the business and professional district.

Elizabeth turned right on Bates and left onto Lompock. Palm trees lined the broad avenue. "What's the address?" she asked.

"Fourteen ten," Jessica said with hardly a glance at the letter on the seat beside her. "That's it up there on the right."

"This looks like a movie studio," Elizabeth remarked as she drove through the gates and stopped to tell the guard that they were going to Building B.

"Maybe they're going to film the discussion group," Jessica suggested as she looked around.

"Maybe," Elizabeth said thoughtfully.

They parked outside the large building marked with the letter *B*.

"Oh, I see some of the other twins for the discussion group over there," Elizabeth said, nodding toward two gorgeous, blond teenage girls lounging against the side of the building. "Good, I'm glad we're not late."

"Me, too." Jessica led the way toward a door on which was posted a typewritten sign. Jessica blocked Elizabeth's view as she scanned the paper.

"What does it say?" Elizabeth asked, trying to peer around her sister.

"Nothing. This is the place, that's all," Jessica said, opening the door quickly, taking Elizabeth's arm, steering her in front of her, and pushing her through.

"Hey, Jess! Don't shove!" *This is getting weird*, Elizabeth thought.

Jessica marched up to the receptionist at the front desk and told her their names.

"Down the hall, and it's the first door on your left. Good luck!" the woman said, smiling at the girls.

"That was an odd thing to say," Elizabeth said. She had a funny feeling, the funny feeling that she *always* got when Jessica was up to something.

Elizabeth heard Jessica's deep breath as they reached the door. "This is it!" Jessica whispered excitedly.

The girls opened the door, entered the large waiting room, and took seats. Elizabeth smiled at two girls about their age who were sitting across from them on a mauve couch. Then she glanced around the room. There were *a lot* of girls their age there. She looked to her right and her left and saw literally dozens of girls *their age*. There were at least *twenty* sets of twins in the room. And they were all *their age*.

Every set of twins looked as if they had just stepped out of the pages of *SuperTeen* magazine. Next to Elizabeth and Jessica, two tall and lanky blondes were reading magazines, their legs crossed identically and their feet bouncing in perfectly synchronized rhythm. Next to this pair were two petite, pretty girls in designer jeans, talking animatedly with another set of girls who looked as if they had just blown in from the beach. This set was wearing matching shorts outfits with coordinated sandals and beach bags.

"Hi." The girl sitting across from Elizabeth greeted her with a perfect smile. "The waiting is horrible, isn't it? You're lucky you arrived just now. The tension in this room has been pretty thick."

"Really?" Elizabeth asked. *For a discussion group?* Elizabeth was becoming more and more suspicious. She turned to mention the strangeness of it all to Jessica. After all, the letter had said there would be a cross-section of participants for a diversity of opinions, but this was about the most nondiverse group Elizabeth had ever seen.

Jessica's attention was on a woman who had just entered the waiting room from another door in the far wall.

"Good afternoon, girls," the woman said.

Elizabeth opened her eyes wide. The woman had the most amazing hairdo she had ever seen. It was twisted into a single, unicorn-type horn on the front of her head and wrapped in multicolored ribbons. More ribbons dangled from her ears and blended with her blouse, which was also a kaleidoscope of ribbons. Her pants were skintight white leather, and her shoes were sequined. *Sequins in the daytime!* Elizabeth resisted the impulse to burst out laughing.

"All right, girls," the woman announced. "I'll call your names, one set at a time, and you can read for the selection committee in the other room. When you're finished, just go on home and we'll call you with the news."

The crowd nodded and murmured. The petite blondes fidgeted in their seats, anticipation lighting their eyes.

Elizabeth glanced over at Jessica's enraptured face. And suddenly the awful truth hit her. This wasn't a discussion group at all.

This was the *Young and the Beautiful* audition!

Jessica had tricked her *again!*

And just when I was about to give in and agree to go to this stupid thing! Elizabeth thought, her face growing hot. *This is the last straw. If she thinks I'm going to just roll over and play dead, she had better think again!*

"Excuse me, sister *dear*," Elizabeth nudged Jessica. "May I have a word with you? In private?"

"Not now, Liz. We don't want to miss our names being called."

"You didn't really think I would go along with this, did you?" Elizabeth hissed.

Jessica smiled sheepishly. Then she turned her attention back to the woman with the unicorn horn.

Elizabeth fumed. Jessica really thought she *had*

gotten away with this! She had sent the letter from the research company herself and dreamed up this elaborate scheme to drag her to the television studio. Elizabeth wanted to kick herself for being so gullible.

With each moment she sat silently, the madder she became. It wasn't just a matter of principles anymore. Now her honor was at stake! There was no way she was going to let Jessica get away with this.

Elizabeth suddenly stood up, drawing the attention of everyone in the room. "I'd like to speak with you, Jessica," she said.

Jessica ignored her and concentrated on the woman, who was addressing the group. The girls around them began talking in hushed tones.

Louder, Elizabeth said, "*Now*, Jess!"

"Later," Jessica whispered.

"There won't be any later," Elizabeth cried, raising her voice. "You've brought me here against my will, and I will no longer submit to your devious, underhanded tactics!"

The woman stopped speaking and looked meaningfully in their direction. The crowd of girls was quiet, too, listening to the Wakefields' exchange.

"What's she doing?" one girl whispered.

"Beats me," her twin replied.

"Shh! Liz!" Jessica begged. "You're making a scene."

But Elizabeth didn't care. She *hoped* she was making a spectacle of them, and she hoped Jessica felt as humiliated by it as she did at having been duped.

41

"I don't care if the whole world hears me," Elizabeth shouted. "You had no right to trick me into coming to Los Angeles. And if you think for one minute I'm going to stay here and pretend to be thrilled about auditioning, then you had better think again!"

She turned and headed for the door. She hadn't gone two steps before Jessica put her hand on Elizabeth's shoulder to stop her.

"Please, Liz," Jessica said to her stiff back. "Don't do this to me! Don't do this to us! We're a team. You can't leave me here alone, stranded!"

"Oh, I'm sure you'll be able to *scam* your way out of it," Elizabeth said. "Maybe you'll even be rescued by one of your famous daytime heroes. As for me, I'm leaving. I'll wait ten minutes for you in the car, and if you don't show up, I'm going home!"

With that, Elizabeth shrugged Jessica's hand off her shoulder and marched, ramrod straight, to the door. She opened it, walked through, and shut it calmly, her dignity intact.

For a full thirty seconds everyone in the room was silent. Jessica watched the door, hoping against hope that Elizabeth would suddenly reappear with a smile on her face and a hearty "Gotcha!"

Finally, she had to face the fact that it wasn't going to happen.

Slowly she turned back to the people in the room, knowing she had to say something. Already she could see heads bending together and hear whispered comments.

42

"Have you ever seen anything so stupid in your life?" one lanky twin asked her sister.

"They really blew it," another twin commented.

Jessica looked at the floor. "I'm sorry," she said softly. "Please excuse my sister. She doesn't usually behave this way. . . ."

Jessica's voice trailed off as she lifted her head, and she saw the woman smile and nod, her beribboned horn bobbing up and down on her head. Then the most amazing thing happened.

The woman started to clap. "Brava!" she said. "Outstanding performance! I couldn't have asked for a better Tiffany and Heather argument, even with a script."

"But our names are Jessica and Elizabeth," Jessica said confusedly.

"Wakefield, right?" she confirmed, checking her list. "Well, congratulations. Tiffany and Heather are the twins you'll be playing in the show—that is, if you're still interested in a week on *The Young and the Beautiful.* That *was* your audition, wasn't it?"

"I can't believe it!" Jessica heard one girl say.

"They pulled it off while we all sat here and watched," another added. "Why didn't *we* think of doing something outrageous like that?"

A chorus of groans filled the room.

Jessica recovered quickly. The impossible *had* happened. The woman had mistaken Elizabeth's outburst for a clever audition ploy. Jessica wasn't about to let the opportunity of a lifetime slip away.

"Of course that was our audition," she said, stepping forward and extending her hand. "I'm Jessica," she added.

43

"I'm Natasha Talbot, casting director for *The Young and the Beautiful*." They shook hands.

"Jessica," Ms. Talbot repeated. "The demure one." She made a note on her clipboard. "You'll play Heather, and Elizabeth can play Tiffany, the more fiery twin."

Jessica laughed silently at the irony of Natasha Talbot's assignment of the roles. If she only knew. . . .

"So you thought our little scene was good?" Jessica asked eagerly, still finding it hard to believe this was really happening.

"It was the best audition I have seen in a lifetime of boring tryouts. You two really have the right chemistry. I'm sorry, girls," she said, addressing the rest of the room. "I've made my decision. Good luck in your other acting endeavors."

Jessica happily followed the casting director into the adjoining studio. Her exit was punctuated by more groans and comments from the twins who were still in the waiting room.

Jessica and Natasha Talbot sat down at a small table.

"Here are your contracts and scripts," she said. "We won't begin taping your episodes until next week, but I'd like you and Elizabeth to become familiar with the cast and the crew and the way we do things around here. That will make it easier when it comes to the actual filming."

"Thank you, Ms. Talbot!" Jessica exclaimed. "I can't wait to meet everyone and learn all about the business. I've always wanted to be an actress!"

"Call me Natasha," she said with an indulgent smile. "With your enthusiasm, I predict you'll go far. But let's take this one step at a time for now."

"Of course," Jessica said more calmly. After all, Natasha thought she was the *demure* twin.

"I'd like to invite you and your sister to visit the set several times during the next week—get used to the activity, the language. In fact, we're having a cast luncheon tomorrow. Why don't you two come? It will give you a chance to meet everyone off set."

"We'll come!" Jessica said quickly. *At least, I'll come. Liz probably won't speak to me for the rest of her life.*

"Wonderful!" Natasha said, standing up. "We'll see you here at eleven o'clock tomorrow."

"I'll—I mean, *we'll*—be there."

Jessica took the contracts and scripts, walked out of the studio, floated past the receptionist, and flew down the hall. She had made it all the way to the parking lot before she crashed back to earth. She crashed the minute she saw Elizabeth sitting in the driver's seat of the car, her expression stony and her arms folded.

"I was just about to leave without you," Elizabeth said, looking pointedly at her watch. She turned the key in the ignition and started the engine.

"I'm glad you didn't," Jessica told her softly. "Something really exciting happened in there after you left."

"I don't want to hear about it!" Elizabeth informed her testily. "You could have met the

45

Queen of England, and it wouldn't impress me a bit!"

"What if I told you that we got the parts of Tiffany and Heather? And how's this for a twist—they want me to play the demure twin and you to play the fiery twin! Isn't that a riot?" Jessica ventured on, undaunted. "You really had everyone fooled in there."

"I wasn't fooling." Elizabeth's tone was frosty.

"You're really good at this, Liz," Jessica plodded on. "I didn't realize what a good actress you were. All we have to do is get Mom and Dad to look over the contracts with us, and we'll jump right into the hottest soap opera in the country!"

Elizabeth put the car in gear and drove out of the parking lot, without even a glance at her twin.

"C'mon, Liz. Don't be so hard on me! We're sisters. You stand up for me, I stand up for you—right?"

"Well, that's true, but—"

"But what, Liz! Listen, this means a lot to me. I *had* to do something drastic to get you here. I know we'll have fun, if you just give it a chance. Admit it, Liz. You haven't exactly been flexible on this issue."

"I actually *had* planned to tell you that I *would* go to the audition with you after all. I was going to tell you after the discussion group," Elizabeth said.

"But that would have been too late!"

"What do you mean, 'too late'? There was no such thing! Anyway, how was I supposed to know when the audition was? You never told me!"

46

"You never asked!" Jessica cried, throwing up her hands. "Oh, what difference does it make now? You were going to do it, and now you've done it. Aren't you even the least bit excited?"

"Maybe later I'll be excited. Right now, I don't want to talk about it anymore."

No matter how much Jessica begged, pleaded, and whined, Elizabeth wouldn't say another word all the way home. Jessica had never seen her sister so mad. How was she ever going to persuade her to change her mind about the show?

Jessica wracked her brain, but by the time they reached home, she still hadn't come up with a good idea. She just had to hope that Elizabeth's "maybe later" meant she might reconsider after she cooled down.

"C'mon, Liz," Jessica pleaded as they were entering the house. "We can work this out, can't we? We've always talked things out before."

"Not this time," Elizabeth said, speaking for the first time since they had left the studio. "I'm through being manipulated by you. Don't even bother trying any more tricks, because the answer is *no!*"

Five

In spite of Elizabeth's resolute attitude, Jessica had recovered most of her good spirits by the time Sam picked her up for their date that night.

"I just *know* there's a way to make her reconsider," she told Sam as they sat across from each other at a table overlooking the ocean at the Beach Café. She lapsed into silence as she gazed out at the perfect Southern California sunset. Oranges, reds, and deep purples stained the horizon. Lost in thoughts about her future acting career, she paid little attention to Sam's rambling talk of the dirt-bike race he was riding in the next day.

"I think I have a good chance of winning," he said. "I've raced against most of these guys before and won."

"Umm," Jessica said.

"The only one I have to worry about is Matt Horn."

"Uh-huh."

"I've been overhauling my bike for a week, ever since last Saturday's race, and I think it's in the best shape it's ever been in."

"That's nice," Jessica mumbled. Her mind was on the luncheon the next day—how she was going to get there, and whether she would meet superstar Brandon Hunter.

"Are you listening to me?" Sam asked sharply. "Jessica!"

"What? Oh, sorry," she said, shining her best smile on him. "I was thinking about the luncheon tomorrow and the people I might meet. I think I'll call Lila and see if her offer still stands to spend the weekend in L.A. at her father's business associate's hotel. She's always trying to get me to go with her. And this way, I'll be in L.A. in case anything else comes up." *Like a date with Brandon*, she thought.

"Jess," Sam said, with a laugh, "I'm beginning to think Elizabeth is right. You *don't* think of anyone but yourself."

"That's not true. I think about you." Jessica smiled and took his hand.

Sam grinned. "Not for the last hour you haven't. I'll bet you don't even know where I'm going or what I'll be doing this weekend while you're off gallivanting around Los Angeles."

"Well, uh . . ." *What was it Sam just said?* Jessica couldn't remember.

"See!" Sam told her triumphantly. "You haven't listened to a word I've said. You know," he added, leaning close, "I can be *just* as exciting as Brandon Hunter any day. Why don't you let me show you . . . ?"

Jessica looked at Sam's handsome face, and suddenly his teasing didn't seem funny. "You're making fun of me," she accused. "You still think I should forget the whole thing, don't you?"

"Well, since you asked . . ."

"I *won't* forget it!" Jessica cried. "Liz is just being stubborn. There's no way I'm going to pass up a week on national television. The least you can do is back me up!"

"I've been trying, Jess," Sam told her softly, "but enough is enough! A guy needs his girlfriend to back *him* up once in a while, too. When was the last time you came out to the track to watch me race?"

"Last weekend," Jessica reminded him triumphantly.

"Only because we went shopping in Santa Barbara afterward," Sam joked. "I think you liked the stores better than my performance."

Jessica shrugged. "I love to shop, what can I say? But I love you, too. Well, maybe not as much as a new sweater."

"Thanks a lot!" Sam said, rolling his eyes. "At least I know where I stand."

Jessica leaned forward. "I think you look pretty good standing . . . or sitting, for that matter."

"It's all a game to you, isn't it, Jess? I just hope you know what you're doing."

Jessica could not tell whether Sam was joking or serious. He was still smiling, but the tone of his voice had changed. Anyway, she was tired of trying to convince him of how important this was to her. She had wanted to have a nice romantic dinner and tell him all about her hopes and dreams, and here he was practically lecturing her.

She tossed her napkin on the table. "I'm ready to go. How about you?"

"Me, too. You know, Jess, maybe you should think about forgetting the whole thing, before you and Liz have a big falling out."

That doesn't even deserve an answer, Jessica thought. All she was doing was trying to make something of her life, and Sam was being so mean.

They barely spoke on the way home. The more Jessica thought about it, the more unfair she felt he was being. She shrugged off his attempts at conversation. So what if she missed a couple of races or a conversation about dirt bikes? This soap opera opportunity was the biggest thing that had ever happened to her. It was far more important than any old dirt-bike race. In fact, she was going to start reading the script the minute she got home.

When Sam dropped her off and sped away without even kissing her good night, Jessica was more than a little angry.

"It would serve you right if Brandon Hunter fell for me," Jessica said to Sam's retreating taillights. "And if I left *you* in the dust!"

"Isn't it lucky that your dad is spending the weekend in L.A. on business?" Jessica remarked to Lila and Amy as they drove into the city the next day.

"What a great way to hang out," Amy said from the back seat. "A whole weekend of shopping and sightseeing without our parents around. What did your parents say when you told them about the luncheon, Jessica?"

Jessica stretched in the seat. "Well, there was kind of a blowup when I told them last night what had happened. I think they were really wavering about whether I should come or not, but I convinced them that I just wanted to meet these people, even if Liz and I don't end up doing the show. And I apologized profusely for being so sneaky."

"That worked?" Amy asked. "Gosh, if I did something like that, my parents would probably ground me for a month!"

"My parents are pretty cool," Jessica said. "And besides, I think they're kind of in favor of us doing the show—for the experience and the money and all that. They're just waiting for Liz to come around."

"By the way, how *are* things with Liz?" Lila asked.

"Terrible. She still isn't speaking to me, and Sam thinks I'm nuts. As far as he's concerned, I should be hanging around the racetrack with him."

"Boys can be very strange," Amy commented. "Barry is always saying crazy things. They ought to listen to themselves once in a while. And have you heard Bruce Patman lately? He's really on a kick about livening up Sweet Valley."

"Bruce is always on a kick about something,"

Jessica said, laughing. "No one takes him seriously."

"That's for sure. I'm glad your dad is going to be in L.A. on business this weekend, Lila. The only reason my parents let me come was because we'd be under Mr. Fowler's watchful eye," Amy said.

"That's a laugh," Lila said. "If we see my dad for five minutes all weekend, I'll be amazed. But we can keep in touch with him by phone," she added, patting the brand-new fuchsia car phone her father had just had installed for her.

"Fine with me," Jessica said. "So long as we let him know where we're going and when we're going to be back, there should be no problem. I can't wait to go to the luncheon."

"I wish I was going with you," Lila said. "That Marcus O'Ryan, who plays Brandon's brother on the show, is pretty cute."

"Just be sure to memorize every word and detail so that you can report back to us," Amy added.

"Will do," Jessica agreed, lounging back against the plush seat of Lila's lime-green Triumph. "You know you can count on me."

Ten minutes later, Lila dropped her off at the studio.

"I'll call you at the hotel when I need you to come pick me up," Jessica said, leaning in the window.

"Try the car phone if we're not there. We'll probably be cruising around someplace, checking out the guys."

"OK. Wish me luck?"

"Have fun!" "Good luck!" "Give Brandon a kiss for me," they called as Lila drove off.

Jessica straightened her black leather miniskirt and tucked a stray piece of her new red blouse into the waistband. She checked her reflection in a window as she walked by, then opened the door to the studio and entered the same lobby that had changed the course of her life only yesterday.

"Hello," she greeted the receptionist. "Remember me? I'm Jessica Wakefield. Where is the cast for *The Young and the Beautiful* holding its luncheon today?"

"Hi, Jessica. I'm Madeline. Welcome aboard!"

"Thanks. I can't wait to meet everyone!"

"The luncheon is up on the roof," Madeline told her. "The elevator's over there."

"Thanks." Jessica headed for the metal doors.

"Where's your sister?" Madeline called after her.

"Liz wasn't feeling well today," Jessica lied.

"I'm sorry to hear that. Tell her I hope she feels better soon."

"I will."

Gratefully, Jessica slipped inside the elevator and pushed the button for the roof. Well, it was true that Elizabeth hadn't been acting like herself lately. Maybe she did have some rare cranky disease. That would explain the strange stubborn streak that had taken over her usually flexible personality.

Once Jessica arrived on the roof, she forgot all about Elizabeth. The sight that greeted her took

54

her breath away. All sorts of beautiful pots spilling with flowers lined the low walls. A buffet table laden with food sat along one wall, and round tables, complete with umbrellas and padded chairs, were arranged in the center of the roof.

But the setting wasn't the most amazing part. Jessica felt as if she had stepped into a garden party scene on *The Young and the Beautiful*. There was Dr. Maples conversing casually with Leticia and Mavis, notorious sisters with steamy story lines. In another corner, Frank and Jed Levensworth were carrying on an animated conversation with the Evanses, a supposedly straight-laced, married couple whom Jessica and the rest of the viewing public suspected of smuggling counterfeit artwork. Marcus O'Ryan, Lila's favorite, was standing at the buffet table, busily filling his plate.

"Jessica! Or is it Elizabeth?" Natasha called out to her. "I'm so glad you could come."

"It's Jessica. Thank you. Everything looks wonderful!" Jessica said.

"Where's Elizabeth?" Natasha asked. "Not still out in the car in a tiff, I hope!" she added with a laugh.

If you only knew, Jessica thought. Aloud she repeated her lie. "Elizabeth isn't feeling herself today. She sends her apologies."

"No problem. You can give her the scoop, hmm? Besides, we want *both* of you in tip-top shape for the shooting next week."

Natasha put her arm around Jessica and guided her to the buffet table. "Grab a plate and find a seat. Then I'll introduce you to some of the cast."

Jessica was left alone at the buffet table for a moment, and she began to fill her plate.

"That's great," said a deep, masculine voice next to her. "She wants you in tip-top shape so that you can be shot next week. Doesn't our lingo strike you as odd?"

Jessica laughed. "It sure does. So far, I'm planning on being shot, gaffed, and gripped. I hope my mother isn't worried."

She turned to face her conversational partner and almost dropped her plate.

Brandon Hunter. The star of the show. The biggest name in daytime TV. In the flesh!

"Hi," she said, hoping her surprise didn't show. "I'm Jessica Wakefield."

"My new amour," Brandon said, bending down and kissing her outstretched hand.

He was so completely gorgeous. Even better looking in person than he was on TV, Jessica decided. And he was *kissing* her hand. Wait until she told Lila and the others!

Jessica flashed him a million-dollar smile when he raised his head. "Funny we should meet like this," she said. "I've been watching you from afar for so long, it seems as though we already know each other."

Brandon's eyelids closed sexily as he looked at her. "I know what you mean," he said huskily. "Would you care to sit down?"

Could he tell that her knees were about to collapse? She actually thought she might be experiencing love at first sight.

"I'd love to," Jessica responded, her eyes never leaving his handsome face. *He's interested, too. I can tell. Other boys have looked at me with that look, and I know it means that they want to get to know me.*

Several people joined them, including Natasha. "Jessica, I'd like you to meet Marve Akins. He's the producer of our show. And this is William Green. He's our director."

"I'm pleased to meet both of you," Jessica said. "I'm really looking forward to working on the show."

"We're happy to have her, aren't we, Brandon?" Marve commented.

"You bet!" Brandon said, touching her elbow as he indicated a nearby table.

They all sat down and began to eat, but Jessica was so excited and so captivated by Brandon's attentions that she could barely swallow a bite of food. He refilled her glass, jumped up and retrieved her napkin when she dropped it accidentally, and told her stories about life on the set.

Brandon had done so many interesting things. Unlike Sam, who only wanted to talk about his bike.

"So have you two heard about your story line yet?" William asked.

"I read the script last night," Jessica said. "It was very interesting." *I left a copy on Elizabeth's desk*, Jessica thought. *I just know that if she picks it up, she'll find it interesting, too.*

"It's one of the most exciting story lines of the whole year," Marve put in. "You two girls will fight over America's number-one bachelor, and by the end of the week, he'll choose one of you to be his lady love. The fans will go crazy over it."

"Jessica's the one who will succeed, and I can

see why," Brandon murmured. "She's already stolen my heart."

Jessica batted her eyelashes and affected a southern accent. "Why, Brandon Hunter, I do believe you're trying to butter me up."

The whole table burst into laughter. Brandon tried to act humble, but his wink gave him away. "Can I help it if I'm hooked on beautiful women?"

Jessica was enjoying the flattery. She liked having gorgeous guys pay attention to her. Besides, it could be very advantageous to her career to cultivate Brandon Hunter's friendship.

Marve, William, and Natasha got into a conversation about lighting during an outdoor scene, but Brandon seemed uninterested.

"So, tell me about yourself, Jessica," he crooned.

"Oh, there's not much to tell," she said. "I'm a junior at Sweet Valley High. I'm a cheerleader. I love to go to the beach and hang out at the mall. Pretty typical stuff. I'm much more interested in *you*."

"Oh, there's not much to tell," Brandon mimicked her. "I'm twenty-two, and I work as an actor on a soap opera. Pretty typical stuff."

"And you're the number-one daytime heartthrob all across America," Jessica added. "You played football in high school and college, where you majored in drama. Your favorite color is red, and your sign is Taurus."

"You must read the tabloids."

"Only the ones that tell the truth," Jessica said with a grin. "It *is* true, isn't it?"

"Well, looking at you in that red blouse, I'd say that my favorite color definitely *is* red, and I *am* a Taurus. But the tabloids *didn't* mention that I'm a championship water skier and an accomplished scuba diver. I love to hang glide and sky dive, too."

"You like to live on the edge," Jessica commented.

"Is there any other way to live?"

"None that I can think of," she agreed. "I've had a few death-defying experiences of my own. There was the time I was taken hostage by a drug smuggler, and—"

"That's very interesting, Jessie," Brandon said quickly. "Did I tell you that I climbed Mount Whitney in January?"

"No! That's incredible!" Jessica replied. Her story could wait.

By the time lunch was over, Jessica had gathered enough gossip about Brandon and the other stars on the show to keep Lila, Amy, and all of her friends back home talking for weeks. Once he got going, Brandon had seemed to talk incessantly about his escapades, and that was fine with Jessica. She was just happy to have had his undivided attention for the whole afternoon.

As the tables were being cleared, Jessica got up and shook hands with the director and the producer. She had hardly spoken to them, but they seemed impressed with her. Especially when William Green had asked her about the contracts, and she had told him that her father, a lawyer, wanted to look them over for a day or two. They all thought that was very wise.

"I'm so happy to have met all of you," Jessica

said. "I'm really looking forward to visiting the set while you're working next week."

"I hope you're not going to run off and disappear like Cinderella," Brandon whispered close to her ear. "Are you busy tonight?"

She shivered in anticipation. The look in his warm brown eyes practically stopped her rapidly beating heart.

"No," she answered, hoping she didn't look too nervous. Of course, she had made plans to go to dinner and a movie with Lila and Amy, but she was sure they would understand.

Brandon leaned a little closer. "I've been invited to a party at Bill Lacey's mansion tonight. You know Bill Lacey, don't you? He sings."

Bill Lacey was only the most famous rock star on the charts at the moment. *He sings*—what a way to put it!

"Yes, I know who he is," Jessica said as calmly as she could.

"Anyway, I'd like you to be my date to his party. He's arranged a private screening of his new unreleased video."

"I'd love to go," Jessica replied, striving for just the right amount of excitement and maturity. "I'm staying at the Belmont Hotel." She was glad that the Belmont was one of the most luxurious hotels in all of Los Angeles. It made her feel sophisticated.

And it seemed that Brandon was impressed by the Belmont, too, because he bestowed another superstar smile on her.

"I'll pick you up at eight."

Speechless with the thrill of it all, Jessica could only nod.

Jessica was about to float away to the elevator when Brandon called her name. He caught up with her and whispered conspiratorially. "I'm not sure whether you brought anything to wear to a gig like this," he said. "But the wardrobe department is at your disposal. C'mon. I'll take you there to pick out something as gorgeous as you are."

Six

"The party is in Beverly Hills," Jessica told Lila and Amy later that afternoon. "Can you believe it? This is the best, the most exciting thing that has ever happened to me. Ever! Did I tell you that the party is at Bill Lacey's mansion?"

"You told us! You told us!" Amy said. "I wish *I* could go. Why don't you take pictures?"

Jessica rolled her eyes. "Then I *would* look like a tourist. I have to try to blend in with the crowd, make some contacts."

"You're so calm," Amy declared. "I'd be a basket case if I was in your place right now. And that jumpsuit! Is that drop dead, or what? The whole wardrobe department to choose from. It's like a fairy tale come true."

"I'd never be able to afford something like this on my own," Jessica agreed as she ran her hand along the red-sequined top and let the silk pants slip through her fingers. "Matching earrings, too," she added, holding up shoulder-length dangling sequins and watching them sparkle in the sunlight coming in through the hotel window.

"I want to be there when he comes to pick you up," Amy said.

"I'll introduce you, no problem," Jessica said.

"No, no. I'll just be hidden discreetly behind a potted palm," Amy told her. "I don't want to be obvious."

"In that case, why don't you hold a newspaper up in front of your face like the spies in old movies do," Jessica teased.

For a second Amy looked as if she were really contemplating Jessica's suggestion.

"I'm kidding, Amy. Just come down with me to the lobby at eight and meet him. Brandon's really nice."

"I'll think about it," Amy finally said.

The telephone rang at that moment. It was Brandon himself on the line.

"What did he say?" Lila asked as Jessica hung up the phone a few minutes later. "He's not backing out, is he?"

"Not at all," Jessica said, trying not to show her relief. For a moment, she, too, had thought the phone call would be to cancel. "He's tied up in a meeting right now, so he's sending his driver to pick me up. I'm going to ride to Bill Lacey's mansion in a limousine!"

For a full five minutes the girls jumped and danced around the hotel room. Jessica was beyond ecstatic. She was delirious with excitement and anticipation.

The only damper on the total perfection of the

evening was the fact that she knew Elizabeth was still against the whole thing, and that if she didn't change her mind, this day and evening would be the only memories Jessica would have of life with *The Young and the Beautiful.* Jessica wished Elizabeth were with her. She just *knew* that her sister would be having as much fun as she was, if she'd only give it a chance.

As Jessica got dressed for the party, her thoughts turned from Elizabeth to her parents. Somewhat to her surprise, they were being very cool about the whole thing. She remembered the conversation they had had earlier in the day, when she had called to ask permission to go to the party.

"Have you mentioned to Ms. Talbot that Liz might not agree to be on the show?" Mr. Wakefield had asked.

"No, I haven't had the chance," Jessica told him. "I keep hoping that Liz will change her mind. These people are really nice. Thanks for letting me come to L.A. to meet them."

"Did you have fun at the luncheon?" her mother had asked from the other phone extension.

"Oh, you should have seen it, Mom! The luncheon was given on the roof! I'll tell you all about it when I get home. What I'm calling for now is to ask permission to go to a party tonight. It's at Bill Lacey's mansion in Beverly Hills. Brandon Hunter is going to take me."

"A date?" her father asked. "Isn't he a little old for you?"

"It's all perfectly innocent, Dad," Jessica had explained. "And lots of other people will be there from the cast. Mr. Lacey's going to be showing his new video, that's all."

"I don't know," Mrs. Wakefield had remarked. "I've read a lot of bad press about these show business parties."

"I think it's going to be fairly tame," Jessica had assured her. "For one thing, it's formal. The TV studio even loaned me an outfit for the evening."

"That was very nice," her mother had said.

"And I'm sure that Natasha Talbot will watch over me. You'd like her. She's like a second mother." *With a horn and ribbons,* Jessica had added silently.

"Just make sure you take enough money for a taxi if you need it," Mr. Wakefield hastened to advise.

"Will do, Dad. And thanks for letting me go. I'll tell you all about it when I get home."

By the time Jessica arrived at the party in her borrowed outfit and limo on loan, she really was feeling like Cinderella going to the ball.

She succumbed to only a moment of panic when the driver dropped her off and she stood alone at the bottom of a long flight of stairs, ogling the columned entry to the Lacey mansion. She wondered if Brandon had already arrived, or if she was going to have to make her entrance alone.

But then, out of the chandeliered entry, her prince emerged, silhouetted in the brilliance of a thousand twinkling lights. "I've been waiting for you," he said, coming down to meet her.

All my life, Jessica added silently.

A moment later, Jessica was led into the swirl

and dazzle of her first Hollywood party. Glamorous people, swanky furniture, priceless works of art, waiters carrying trays of food, and reporters with flashbulbs popping created a kaleidoscope of color and sound.

The parade of famous faces dazzled her. Everywhere she looked, she saw another three-dimensional version of one of her TV, movie, or music industry favorites.

But of all the famous people there, it was obvious that Brandon Hunter was the most sought-after, the biggest celebrity. And she was his date. It was unbelievable!

"Jessica, I'd like you to meet our host, Bill Lacey," Brandon said as a tall man wearing an expensive-looking, custom-tailored leather outfit came up to them.

"It's a pleasure, Jessica," Bill Lacey said, extending his right hand. With his left, he slapped Brandon on the back. "I have to hand it to you, old chum. You always bring the prettiest women."

Jessica tried to forget about all the *other* parties and the *other* pretty women that Bill Lacey was referring to and concentrate on the compliment.

"You have a beautiful home, Mr. Lacey," she said.

"Call me Bill."

"I love the chandelier in your entryway . . . Bill."

"I picked that up in Norway," Bill said. "Feel free to roam around and take a look. There are some Hummels in the library that I just brought back from Germany—turn of the century, I think—cost a bundle. Don't really like those Hummels, but my financial planner says they're a good investment."

"I'll have to take a look at them," Jessica said, beginning to feel more at ease. These people weren't snobs. Here she was talking with a famous rock star, and he was as down to earth as anyone else—anyone else with a multimillion-dollar mansion and several million dollars' worth of collectibles, that is.

Of course, she reminded herself, she should have remembered that from the time she met rock star Jamie Peters, who was her friend Andrea Slade's father. He was a regular guy, too. In fact, the way Mr. Peters worried about his daughter made him seem *a lot* like Jessica's own father!

"Could I get your autograph for my best friend, Lila?" Jessica asked. "We're both big fans of yours."

"Sure," Bill said. "I've got some compact discs over on the table. Help yourself to one of those, too."

"Thanks. I know she'll appreciate it."

Without warning, a photographer jumped in front of them and said, "Smile!" All smiled, and she snapped their picture.

Brandon excused himself for a moment, and a second later Bill introduced her to another couple. By the time an hour had passed, she was feeling very comfortable in her new environment.

It was a good thing, too, because Brandon kept running off to talk with one business partner or another and leaving her to fend for herself.

But Jessica understood. He was a busy, famous star, and she was just a high school student. As

Jessica watched him work his way through the room, she decided that she could get used to this life—money, power, stunning clothes, and famous people treating her as if she were one of them. And the flashbulbs just kept popping. It seemed that every time Brandon came around, there was a photographer on his tail.

What a life!

During a lull in the action, as Jessica was gazing around the room looking for her date, a young man in Bermuda shorts and a wild floral-print shirt came up to her. "Hi," he said. "I'm Steve Limbo. I'm the bass player in Bill's band. You're looking a little lost."

Jessica smiled. "Not lost exactly. I'm here with Brandon Hunter, and I was just wondering where he had gone off to."

"I saw him in the study a while ago with Marve Akins. It looked like they were into a pretty heavy discussion."

"The story of my life," Jessica sighed dramatically, turning her flirting skills on Steve.

"My gain," Steve said gallantly. "So you're one of the new twins on Brandon's show?"

"You follow the soaps?" Jessica asked.

"Sure. I watch them all the time in the hotel room during the day. You know we don't go on until night."

"Yeah, I know. But I thought you'd be busy rehearsing, not watching the soaps!"

"That, too," Steve said, smiling. Then he glanced around at the crowd. "Pretty wild party, huh?"

"It'll probably be my first and last," Jessica said

honestly. "But I'm really glad I got to come to this one. I've met a lot of nice people."

Steve grinned. "I wouldn't be too sure about that prediction. The part about your first and last party, I mean. You seem to fit in real well. If this is the place you want to be and the set you want to be with, I'm sure you'll be back."

Jessica smiled happily. "Thanks for the vote of confidence!" she said.

Brandon approached them, a photographer in tow. "Hi, Steve. Thanks for keeping *my* girl entertained. I haven't been a very good date tonight."

"You've been fine," Jessica said. "I know you have business to attend to." She was getting used to the cameras and the photographers that seemed to dog his every step.

Steve winked and walked away, murmuring something about Brandon being luckier than he knew. But Jessica had already turned her attention back to Brandon.

Up on the stage at the end of the ballroom, a screen rolled down and Bill Lacey's newest video began to play. A cheer went up from the crowd.

"Say, Jess," Brandon said, leaning close to be heard over the music. "I've been such a poor date that I'd like to make it up to you. Would you care to go with me to a movie preview tomorrow afternoon?"

"I'd enjoy that," Jessica said. "But I'll have to clear it with my friends, since we were planning to be home in the early afternoon. There's school on Monday, you know."

"Let your friends go on home. I promise that I'll bring you straight home to Sweet Valley at a decent hour. I'll even call your parents and set it up, if you'd like."

"That's OK," Jessica said. "I'll call my parents. I'm sure it will be fine. But I know they'll want to meet you when you bring me home."

"I'd like to meet them, too," Brandon said, putting his arm around her and smiling for the nearest camera. "Would you like to stop by the wardrobe department again for a new outfit?"

Jessica smiled back. "I'd love to. By the way, have I told you lately that I'm having the time of my life?"

"I'm glad to hear it," Brandon said, his eyes twinkling. "I hope there are even better times to come."

By the time Sunday was over, Jessica was exhausted.

First, she had called her parents. Lila and Amy had gone home, then she and Brandon had gone to the premiere—which was even more glamorous and exotic than she could have hoped for.

After that, she and Brandon had driven back to Sweet Valley, and she had sat through her parents' meeting with him. Brandon had really charmed them. He was so polite and proper.

Thankfully, Elizabeth had made herself absent. Jessica was still hoping to change her mind, and it would have been horrible if Elizabeth had decided to tell Brandon to his face just what she thought about soap operas.

Jessica was definitely exhausted. After Brandon left, she went to her room and crashed.

By Monday morning, Jessica had regained her usual energy. She rushed to school, eager to break her news to the entire student body.

But Jessica's news was all over Sweet Valley High before she even arrived. "Look, Jessica," Lila cried the minute she saw her get out of the Fiat in the parking lot. "Your picture is all over the front page of *National News and Hollywood Snoop.* You're a celebrity!"

Quickly Jessica scanned the article. The title, "Love Match for Soap Star?" stood out in bold type above a picture of Brandon leaning close to Jessica. It almost looked as if they were kissing! The story went on to explain that Jessica and her twin sister, Elizabeth, had just been chosen for plum roles on *The Young and the Beautiful,* and it speculated about their story line and the possible conclusion, given the *obvious* attraction between Brandon and his new on screen "amour."

"It's a good thing my parents met Brandon yesterday and found out that he's just a nice guy," Jessica remarked as she continued to read the second article. "Otherwise this news might have come as quite a shock."

"You're telling me," Lila said. "How's Liz taking it? Any improvements in her attitude?"

"No such luck." Jessica sighed. "I haven't even seen her since I got back from L.A. She was out with Todd yesterday when Brandon brought me home, and then I fell asleep. She had already left for school when I got up this morning. I think she's avoiding the issue *and* me."

"She can't avoid it now," Lila said, pointing to the paper. "The whole world knows."

"I'm hoping the fact that it's in print will convince her that she can't back out," Jessica said.

Throughout the rest of the day Jessica was swamped with questions and congratulations. She wondered if Elizabeth was receiving the same treatment, but she saw her twin only once, as she and Enid ducked into the rest room.

After school, Jessica and some friends headed over to the Dairi Burger to discuss the Wakefields' sudden fame over several giant plates of fries.

Elizabeth and Todd didn't show up, even though Jessica had left a note in her sister's locker inviting them.

"I wish she would see the light," Jessica whispered to Lila as everyone crowded into the after-school hangout. "I don't have much time left. I know one thing, though. I'm not going to give up!"

Just then, Winston came over and handed her a napkin. "May I have your autograph please?" he asked.

Jessica loved being the center of attraction. "Of course you may," she replied graciously. She signed with a flourish and handed the napkin back to him.

"Thanks. I'm trying to give you practice for when you're a star," Winston informed her.

The others gathered around, and Jessica told them what all of the stars had been wearing at the party and the premiere.

"I'd like to see the stars in person," Terri said. "Their pictures are always so perfect, but it makes me wonder how much of that is real and how much is done with makeup and trick photography."

"I don't know. The pictures of *me* that were published turned out pretty well, and no one did anything special," Jessica commented with a laugh. "Except maybe follow us around and pop flashbulbs in our faces whenever we weren't ready. Hey, let me tell you about how Bill Lacey asked me to call him Bill and told me I had the run of his house."

Suddenly she felt a tap on her shoulder. "Hello, Jessica," Sam said, running a hand through his thick blond hair.

"Oh, hi, Sam," Jessica said brightly. "Sit down. I was just about to tell everyone more about this party I went to in Beverly Hills."

She took a breath and continued. "I think there must have been fifty tables of food, and at least a hundred waiters and waitresses wandering around with trays. There was an ice sculpture of a dolphin—that's Bill Lacey's logo for his band—in the middle of the living room. It was ten feet high, I'm sure. And everywhere I looked I saw a painting or a metal sculpture by the original artist. Everything was genuine!"

"Can you imagine how much that party must have *cost*?" Neil said. "I mean, *my* allowance wouldn't pay for it, that's for sure!"

"Mine neither," Ken remarked. "Hey, everyone! Come over to my house. We'll have generic hot dogs!"

"Well, if you think the party I'm describing was fantastic, you should have seen what people were wearing and the spread at the premiere Brandon took me to on Sunday!"

"Was it limousines and red carpets, just like at the Academy Awards?" Maria asked.

"It was *just* like that," Jessica said. "People were wearing so many jewels, the place looked like a lighted Christmas tree. And the gowns must have cost a fortune. The one I was wearing was worth three thousand dollars, but I'm sure that was nothing compared to the gowns some of the stars wore."

"You all don't mind if I steal my *girlfriend* away for a second, do you?" Sam interrupted Jessica's monologue to address the group. "Jess, I really need to talk to you. It's important."

"Sure, Sam. What's up?"

"In private," Sam added.

Jessica excused herself and led him to a back booth and sat down. "That was very rude of you, Sam," she said, smiling and kissing him hello. "I was in the middle of a story."

"I'm sorry to cramp your style, Jessica. I just thought you might want to spend some time with your boyfriend."

"Well, of course I do." Jessica shrugged. "It's just that I've been rather busy."

"I hope not too busy for *me*," Sam said softly. "Let's go out tonight, Jess. I've missed you."

"Sam, I'd really like to. Really, I would," Jessica said, laying a hand on his arm. "But you should see this mountain of homework I have. Spending the weekend in L.A. put me more behind than usual."

74

"We could go to Guido's. You have to eat," Sam reasoned.

Jessica thought about it for a moment, but finally she shook her head. "No, I can't. After all, if I expect to be a TV star, I have to make some sacrifices in my social life."

"Just your social life with me," Sam retorted. "I guess it's hard to make time for *little people* when you have such *big people* like Brandon Hunter to squire you around."

"I didn't mean it that way, Sam," Jessica said with concern. "You just don't understand. If I want to make it in show business, I need to be out there networking and being seen by all the right people. Who knows? At one of these parties or premieres, I might meet an agent and be on my way to the top!"

"No, I guess I don't understand. Maybe I never will. I came in here to be with my girlfriend, but I've found a totally different person—someone who's climbing the ladder to stardom and leaving the people who love her behind," Sam said.

Before Jessica had a chance to reply, Sam got up and walked out of the restaurant.

That's not fair, Jessica thought as she watched him disappear beneath the exit sign, leaving behind only the sound of the jingling bell. What was going wrong lately? Sam certainly didn't seem to be on her side in this. The other night at the restaurant, he had told her to forget her dreams, and now he had accused her of paying more attention to her career than to him. Was he just jealous, or was it something bigger? As far as Jessica could see, Elizabeth and Sam were both having the same problem. Neither of them could be flexible for *one little week* out of their lives!

And he calls me selfish! she fumed silently as she walked back to join the group. *What good is a boyfriend if he can't be supportive of my career?*

Seven

"Elizabeth?" Jessica called softly from the door to her room early the next morning. "Could we talk for a moment?"

Elizabeth hesitated. "I guess. What's up?"

"Liz, I know you think I've gone too far this time, and maybe I have," Jessica cajoled. "But won't you reconsider? It's only a week out of your life, and it would mean so much to me."

Elizabeth stood up from her desk and crossed the room to where Jessica was standing. "You *have* gone too far this time, Jess. I told you, I had been thinking of going along with your plan at one point, but when you went behind my back with that discussion group thing—well, it was just too much."

"But the papers have already announced our acceptance. The publicity is rolling. We can't back out now," Jessica reasoned.

"I won't do it!" Elizabeth repeated. "Even if it

means every gossip rag in the country has to print a retraction!"

"I'm getting desperate," Jessica told Lila later that day in the cafeteria. "It was one thing to tell the soap people that Liz was sick and couldn't come to the luncheon. But I'm not going to be able to play *both* of us onscreen!"

"I really thought Liz would have folded by now," Lila said as she opened her designer lunchbag and laid out her lunch. "I don't understand why she's being so stubborn."

"Me, neither. Unless I can get her to change her mind, I don't stand a chance with *The Young and the Beautiful*, or with Brandon. I know that he's interested in me right now mainly because I'm making a guest appearance on his show. I need to see him more and more in order to convince him that our relationship is worth pursuing outside the studio."

"You're really hung up on this guy, huh?"

"Not hung up, exactly. Not yet. I just see the possibilities. Not only is he cute, and nice, and single, but right now he's my ticket to being seen in Hollywood," Jessica remarked.

"What about Sam?" Lila asked. "You two don't seem to be getting along very well lately."

"I don't know what's wrong with him, Lila," Jessica remarked as she munched on an apple. "He *has* kind of been giving me the hands-off treatment ever since I started talking about trying out for the show. It's like he's jealous or something."

"Wouldn't you be jealous if *your* girlfriend were

going out to places you could never afford to take her with the most eligible bachelor in Hollywood?" Lila asked, quirking her eyebrow.

Jessica bit her lip. "But going out with Brandon is all just for fun . . . and contacts."

"You're not falling for him—even a little?"

"Well," Jessica said with a grin, "maybe a little. But you know, it would serve Sam right for being so rotten about all of this. Do you know that he accused me of being selfish and self-centered? He told me the other night that I should just give the whole thing up!"

"That doesn't sound like Sam," Lila commented. "Maybe he *is* jealous."

"Well, I don't have time to worry about his attitude right now. I have more important things to worry about—like getting Liz to change her mind."

Amy came up to them right then and plopped down on the opposite bench. "Have you seen the latest edition of *The Oracle*?" she asked, spreading it out in front of them. "Look, there's a whole spread on student activities. There are pictures of us at cheerleading practice, Jess. And here you are, Jessica, our illustrious president, running a meeting of Pi Beta Alpha."

"I saw that, too," Lila said. "Elizabeth really did a wonderful job. She even made the Chess Club sound interesting!"

Jessica looked at her sister's two-page spread in the school newspaper. Suddenly, a smile lit up her face. "I've got it!" she exclaimed.

"Got what?" Lila asked.

"What is it that Liz wants more than anything else in the world?"

"Besides Todd?"

Jessica laughed, suddenly feeling very good. "Right, besides Todd. She wants to write for a big newspaper, a paper like the *Los Angeles Times*. I've just thought of a plan that will allow her to write for the *Times* and that'll force her into doing the soap!"

All ears, the girls leaned closer as Jessica outlined her plan.

"It's crazy," Lila said afterward. "But I have to admit, it just might work."

Amy shook her head. "I've got to hand it to you, Jess. *This* is one of your best!"

Later that afternoon, Jessica hurried to arrive home before Elizabeth. On her sister's typewriter she composed a letter to the editor of the *Los Angeles Times* explaining that she and her sister had been selected to appear on *The Young and the Beautiful*. She asked if he would be interested in a series of articles about their experiences working on the show.

Then she gathered copies of some of Elizabeth's best work, including the spread on student activities, and rushed down to her father's study to make copies of them on his copy machine.

Half an hour later, she was ready. She looked over Elizabeth's new portfolio and smiled with satisfaction. Then she called Lila.

"I don't have any time to lose. The signed contracts are due back to the casting director by the end of the week," Jessica explained. "Will you cover for me while I drive to L.A.? I want to deliver this letter and Liz's clips in person to the newspaper. Then I'll follow up tomorrow with a phone call. I just wish I had a set of wheels that I wasn't afraid would break down halfway there!"

"No problem," Lila agreed. "For the next few hours, as far as anyone knows, you're at my house swimming. And if you have a problem with the Fiat, call me. I'll come pick you up, and no one will have to know."

"Thanks, you're a pal. I owe you one."

"I know. And don't worry—I'll collect."

"Mom," Elizabeth said when her mother arrived home from work on Wednesday afternoon. "What do you *really* think about this whole soap opera thing?"

"I think that I see a conflict between my two daughters that isn't being resolved very easily," Mrs. Wakefield replied. "Do you want to talk about it?"

"I just wish Jessica could understand my feelings," Elizabeth said. "I really hate the way soap operas portray women and relationships. It's the same problem I had with the Miss Teen Sweet Valley Pageant. The sponsors and judges expected the contestants to parade around in bathing suits and tight-fitting formals, and the personality part of the contest was just a big joke. The questions the judges asked made the contestants sound stupid no matter *how* intelligently they answered them."

"I think Jessica understood that by the end," her mother said, filling two glasses of water and sitting down at the kitchen table.

"But here she goes again, Mom!" Elizabeth

cried. "Have you ever heard the dialogue the women characters on the soaps are given? They never use their brains! They misunderstand everything that everyone tells them, and they jump to absurd conclusions about the very people that they should *know* they can trust. It makes me sick to watch them."

"Well, you really do have a problem, then. But look, Liz, I know you came to your sister's rescue during the pageant by standing in for her. You also did that interview on the Eric Parker talk show when Jessica couldn't make it. I can see where you could feel as if you've done enough."

Elizabeth sipped her water thoughtfully. "Jessica doesn't see it that way. She thinks I owe her one because of the way she stood up for me after Kris Lynch told all those lies about me."

"Yes, she did do that," her mother said. "I guess you have a lot more thinking to do. I just want you to know that whatever you decide, Dad and I will respect your decision."

"Thanks, Mom," Elizabeth said. She rose from the table and headed for her room. "You know," she said, turning back when she reached the door, "things were easier when we were little kids."

Mrs. Wakefield laughed. "Isn't that the truth!"

"So my parents have given us their permission, but they're letting me make up my own mind," Elizabeth told Todd, Enid, and Hugh on Wednesday evening over their double-date picnic dinner on the beach. "I feel as if I'm really being rotten about all this."

"I don't think you're being rotten at all," Enid said. "Sometimes Jessica goes a little overboard about things. Remember the Good Friends? I thought she'd take things slower after that disaster."

"No such luck. Do you know that she's been out with Brandon Hunter twice now?" Elizabeth commented. "I mean, he came by the house and met my parents and all, but I still wonder about him. I've got a feeling that he's using Jessica. Why else would a twenty-two-year-old superstar suddenly become infatuated with a sixteen-year-old high school student? And poor Sam. I think they've had a falling out."

"You're really worried about her, aren't you?" Todd asked.

"With Jessica, I'm never *not* worried," Elizabeth responded.

Todd took Elizabeth's hand. "None of us thinks you're being unfair. Don't let her pressure you."

"Thanks. It's nice to know that someone agrees with me. Jessica has the entire rest of the world on her side."

The four friends ate their submarine sandwiches in companionable silence. After a while Elizabeth spoke up. "Oh, I almost forgot to tell you guys. There *is* a bit of good news on the horizon. My parents have finally decided to seriously consider that Jeep idea."

"Does Jessica know? She must be ecstatic." Todd grinned.

"No. My dad told me this morning at breakfast, but he didn't mention it to Jess because she's been off in ga-ga land ever since this soap thing began.

He wants me to meet him at the Jeep dealer later. Would you all like to come along?"

"I can't," Enid said. "I stopped studying for my Spanish test just long enough to eat tonight."

"Me, too," Hugh told them. "Tons of homework."

"Well, I'd better go," Todd teased. "Someone has to keep you from going overboard and choosing something with rhinestone stripes and a gold tailpipe."

Elizabeth giggled. "Funny, I believe that's the one Jess wants."

Todd laughed, too. "I'm not surprised."

The four friends quickly finished their dinner and parted company. Todd and Elizabeth drove to the Jeep dealer in the Fiat and were walking around admiring the new Jeeps when Mr. Wakefield arrived.

"I'm almost afraid to ask, but which one was it that Jessica had her heart set on?" Mr. Wakefield asked.

Elizabeth pointed to the model in the center of the showroom floor. It was black with glittery purple trim.

"And which one do you like?" he asked.

Elizabeth led them to the other side of the lot, where a royal blue Jeep with silver trim stood sedately next to its flashier brothers.

At that point the salesman walked up to them and handed Mr. Wakefield his card. "I'm Dan," he said. "May I show you anything in particular?"

"Do you have a brochure on this model?" Elizabeth asked. "I notice that it seats four, maybe five. What kind of gas mileage does it get? Is it available in a basic version without all the fancy striping, piping, and trim?"

"Have you done this before?" Dan asked, his smile widening. "I rarely have customers who know my job better than I do."

Everyone laughed.

"You had better not try any slick sales talk on Elizabeth here," Mr. Wakefield warned him good-naturedly.

"OK, I tell you what," Dan said. "I won't act like a typical salesman. You can ask all the questions you want, and I'll answer them to the best of my ability without an ounce of pressure. Deal?"

"Deal," Elizabeth said. "But I haven't signed anything yet, remember that."

Dan laughed again. "No problem. Here, let me show you what this blue one features, then we'll go up or down from there, depending on your price range."

Elizabeth smiled and took Todd's hand as the four of them stepped closer to the Jeep. Dan explained the size of the engine. "It's a high-output 195 horsepower—the most powerful Jeep engine available."

Then the salesman pointed out the gas mileage ratios for both town and highway driving and the four-wheel capabilities for zipping around on the beach or up in the mountains.

"And it has all the comfort features, too—tilt wheel, cruise control, and most important for those Friday night dates, a removable top."

Todd winked at Elizabeth. "That sounds like fun," he said.

"Let's open the hood," she said, winking back. "Is there easy accessibility to the engine for regular maintenance?"

"I get tired of those fancy engines with electronically bypassed this and that," Dan said. "That's one of the main reasons I like Jeeps. With a little knowledge, anyone can learn to maintain them."

"The girls take care of all their own oil changing, points, plugs, et cetera," Mr. Wakefield said. "How does this engine look to you, Liz?"

"I think we can handle it, Dad. It's a straight six, isn't it?" She put her head under the hood. "Yeah, the spark plugs are all visible, and it shouldn't be any trouble to get to the oil filter or the transmission fluid."

Then Mr. Wakefield asked the price of both the black-and-purple fantasy Jeep on the other side of the lot and the blue one in front of them.

Dan told him the factory invoice and the dealer markup.

Elizabeth and Mr. Wakefield had identical frowns in place when he was finished. "I think that's too much to pay, Dad," Elizabeth said. "Maybe we should look at used cars."

"I'd like to get you something fairly new," Mr. Wakefield said. "Something with the warranty still intact. Life is easier for a few years that way."

Dan smiled and motioned for them to follow him to the back lot. "We have a shipment of new/used Jeeps that just came in yesterday. One of them might be just what you want."

"What do you mean, 'new/used'?" Todd asked.

"They were rentals for a year. Impeccable maintenance, better than most car owners perform.

None of them has more than fifteen thousand miles on it, and they're in great condition. In fact, any new bugs they might have had originally have been worked out by now, and all of them run great. The best part is the price: four thousand dollars less than the new ones."

"Let's take a look," Mr. Wakefield said enthusiastically.

Walking down the rows of new/used Jeeps, Dan stopped at a black one with chrome trim. "This one might be a good compromise," he said. "It has all the safety features that you would want, but none of the fancy extras. It's just a good, all-round transportation vehicle." He grinned and added, "With class."

"I like this one, Dad," Elizabeth said excitedly, leaning over to peer into the interior. "And I think Jess would like it, too."

"It's clean inside and out, even the engine," Todd mentioned. "No scratches on the body."

"Would you like to take it for a test drive?" Dan asked.

"Yes, we would," Mr. Wakefield replied.

Elizabeth found that she liked driving the sporty little Jeep Wrangler even more than the Fiat. It responded well to steering and had good pickup from a dead stop.

When they arrived back at the dealership, though, she wisely acted hesitant. "It's still a lot to pay for a *used* vehicle," she told Dan. "And my sister and I will be contributing to the purchase price. What can we do to bring the price down?"

Dan shook his head, but the tone of his voice demonstrated his respect. "I knew this would happen the minute you asked for a brochure," he said.

Elizabeth grinned. "So what about the price?" she asked again.

"Not going to give me an inch, are you?" Dan said with a laugh.

"Probably not," Elizabeth replied, her eyes twinkling.

"Well, hey," Dan said as he led them into his office, "if you ever need a summer job, we could use you on *our* side."

Elizabeth glanced at her father and Todd as they followed Dan into the dealership showroom. "I'll think about it," Elizabeth told Dan.

Dan excused himself to go over to the credit desk to pick up some papers.

"Keep up the good work," Mr. Wakefield whispered when he was out of earshot. "Dan seems like a nice person, but you still have to be tough as nails when you cut a car deal."

"It's a good-looking Jeep, and it runs well," Todd said, leaning close to Elizabeth. "If you could just knock another thousand dollars or so off of the asking price, I think it would be a good buy."

"I think so, too," Mr. Wakefield added as he saw Dan coming back to join them. "OK, gang. Let's do it!"

An hour later, Elizabeth, Todd, and Mr. Wakefield had negotiated the best deal possible, including a trade-in on the Fiat. Dan was groaning over his loss of commission, and Mr. Wakefield was patting Elizabeth on the back for her perseverance.

Elizabeth and Todd took a spin in the new vehicle on the way home, then parked it in the Wakefields' garage.

"I love it," Elizabeth told him. "And Jess will be so excited. Maybe it will take her mind off show business for a while."

"I doubt that," Todd said. "But there's always hope."

Eight

When Jessica discovered the new set of wheels that night, she was beside herself with joy. She wasted no time before calling all of her friends and offering to drive them around after school the next day. And of course, she had to take it for a test drive around the neighborhood herself.

"Need a ride home?" Todd asked Elizabeth on Thursday afternoon as they watched Jessica drive off with Lila, Amy, and Barry in her new status symbol.

"Thanks. I believe I do." Elizabeth laughed. "I guess I'll get a chance to drive it in a couple of weeks, when the newness wears off."

"Or when Jessica runs out of money for gas," Todd added with a chuckle.

The phone was ringing when Elizabeth let herself into the house fifteen minutes later. She ran to answer it as Todd brought in all of their stuff.

"May I speak with Elizabeth Wakefield, please?" the male voice on the other end of the line asked. "This is Rodney Grant, the Lifestyle editor at the *Los Angeles Times* calling."

"Mr. Grant," she said, puzzled. "This is Elizabeth Wakefield. How may I help you?"

"Ms. Wakefield, may I say first how impressed I am with your writing ability. I've read several articles of yours, including your most recent roundup of school activities for *The Oracle*. It's rare to find someone so young with such style and fluidity."

"Why, thank you," Elizabeth said, a bit confused. How in the world had Rodney Grant found out about her work? She knew that editors kept up with different professional writers' work, but she couldn't imagine that editors from the *Los Angeles Times* had time to scour high school newspapers. And yet wasn't it amazing that he had called, since she had long harbored a desire to write for his paper!

"I've long read and admired the *Los Angeles Times*," Elizabeth told him. "I like the way you tell it like it is, without a bunch of needless speculation and embellishment. I particularly like the Lifestyle section. People enjoy reading about their community."

"I'm glad you feel that way," Mr. Grant said. "And by the way, congratulations on you and your sister landing the roles of Tiffany and Heather on *The Young and the Beautiful*. I *would* like to have you do the series of articles you proposed about your experience on the show. I think our readers would appreciate your down-to-earth attitude as well as the local-girls-make-good angle."

"But . . ." Elizabeth began to protest. Suddenly it was all falling into place. Jessica had done it again! Somehow she had impersonated Elizabeth and proposed a series of articles to the *Los Angeles Times*.

Before she had a chance to explain that the series of articles was not her idea and that she wasn't even planning to be on the show, Mr. Grant went on as if her acceptance were assured. And of course, what else would he think, since he assumed that Elizabeth had sent him her articles and had *asked* to do the story?

"Deadlines for the Lifestyle section are Mondays, Wednesdays, and Fridays at noon. You may send your articles in on disk or fax or deliver them in manuscript form. I would like at least two articles, perhaps three—we'll see how it goes. And as for payment . . ."

He named a sum that left Elizabeth stunned.

"That's very generous," she said. "Thank you. I'll do my best."

"Good luck on the show. I'm looking forward to meeting and working with you," Mr. Grant said before he hung up.

"Me, too," Elizabeth whispered to the dial tone. "You're never going to believe this." Elizabeth turned to Todd. "It appears that Jessica has finally got me where she wants me. I think your girlfriend is going to be a soap opera star."

*   *   *

The minute Jessica walked in the door, Elizabeth confronted her. "How dare you go through my articles and send them to that editor at the *L.A. Times?*"

"Oh, did they call you? Did they offer you the job? You deserve it, you know. You're such a good writer."

"Whether I deserve it or not isn't the point, is it? I have to hand it to you, Jess. You finally figured out the one thing that might convince me to be on that stupid show—a chance to write for a big-city paper."

"Did it work?" Jessica asked anxiously, her fingers crossed behind her back.

Elizabeth didn't answer her right away. Instead, she said, "You knew I wouldn't be able to pass up the chance of a lifetime like this. Writing for Rodney Grant could be the launch of my own career, and the published articles would look *very* good in my clip book."

"That's right," Jessica assured her. "All you'd have to say from now on is, 'I've written a series of articles for the *L.A. Times,*' and you'd have no problem selling articles anywhere else."

"Well, I don't know if it would be *that* easy, but having a few credits at the *Times* couldn't *hurt* my career."

"I've suffered enough. *Please* don't keep me in so much suspense!" Jessica wailed. "Does this mean you'll do the show?"

Elizabeth sighed dramatically. Then she grinned. "Oh, Jess, you're such a goof! I've never seen you so crazy about doing something. I mean, we're talking seriously sneaky here, to get me to do this. All of your effort has to be worth something. Of course I'll do the show!"

"Oh, Liz!" Jessica said, leaping up in the air and doing one of her cheerleader jumps. Then she grabbed Elizabeth and hugged her. "We're going to have so much fun!"

In fact, Elizabeth was surprised by how much fun visiting the set actually was.

"This is fascinating!" Elizabeth exclaimed Friday after school. The twins had driven to Los Angeles in their new Jeep and arrived on the set as the cast was rehearsing for Monday's show.

Her writer's instinct quickly noticed that there wasn't much glamour to the workings. What she did notice was how smoothly the process of videotaping the show went because everyone knew what his or her job was and did it without question. She zeroed in on the mechanics of it all.

"So what does a gaffer do, anyway?" she asked Ron, one of the crew.

"The chief gaffer, or the head production manager, is in charge of all the lighting, sets, and scenery," Ron said, adjusting his headset. "I'm the person who makes sure it looks like daytime or nighttime, like inside or outside. We have to have lights no matter where we shoot."

"That's a pretty big job," Elizabeth observed as she jotted down his explanation on her pad.

"I have my best boys and grips to help me," Ron said. "They're basically production assistants, and they wear several hats. We set up and tear down the scenery, and we hang lights, like that Cyc strip over there that's lighting the background, and the Lekos." He pointed to another bright bulb. "That's a focusable spot for special effects. And then we have Fresnels and Scoops. Let me show you what they do."

"Gets complicated," Elizabeth said a while later after she had written down explanations of the different lights and their uses. "You know, when I read the credits at the end of movies, I've always wondered who all of those funny-sounding titles belonged to. I'm sure other people do, too. I think my first article will explain the different jobs of the crew."

"It's nice to see someone interested in the people who make it happen, for once. After all, the stars have the easy job—all they have to do is smile in front of the cameras! Let me introduce you to Pete. He's the head cameraman. Boy, does he have some stories to tell!"

While Elizabeth was interviewing the camerapeople, sound technicians, and the stage manager, all of whom were connected to the control room by intercom headsets and took their instructions straight from the director, Jessica was hanging around with the cast. Finally Elizabeth wandered over to meet the people she was supposed to love and hate onscreen for the next week.

"This is my sister, Elizabeth," Jessica gushed to Brandon.

"You two really are quite identical, aren't you," Brandon commented.

Very smart, Brandon, Elizabeth thought, barely

95

suppressing a smile. *That's one of the main reasons we were hired.* "Pleased to meet you," she said instead, extending her hand.

"Make sure *one* of them wears something like a necklace so that I can tell them apart onstage," Brandon insisted, brushing aside her greeting.

Jessica then introduced Elizabeth to Marve Akins, William Green, and Natasha Talbot.

"They'll be wearing different clothes," Natasha told Brandon, picking up on the suggestion that he had made a moment before. "And their characters are very different."

"Just put a necklace on Jessica so that I don't make any mistakes on camera," Brandon repeated.

"Fine," Natasha said, writing down Brandon's request.

Elizabeth thought Brandon was being slightly rude, even given his star stature, but she noticed that Jessica was gazing at him adoringly.

Suddenly Brandon smiled. "So I hear that you're doing a series of articles on the show," he said to Elizabeth. "I hope you're planning to interview *me*."

"Of course I am," Elizabeth replied sweetly. "But my first article is going to be on the people behind the scenes. Can I catch you later for the star's-eye view?"

"Sure can," Brandon remarked distractedly. He was already looking off toward one of the sets.

"Thanks," Elizabeth said. "How about tomorrow?"

"Anytime!" he said, still not looking at her.

Elizabeth turned back to Natasha, Marve, and William. "What do we do first?" she asked.

"We'll hold a special rehearsal on Sunday afternoon to familiarize you two with the way we do things around here," William said.

"The general procedure will be rehearsal early each morning, concurrently with filming. We'll film your scenes as early as possible in the day so that you can get back to school," Marve said.

"Then the shows will air each afternoon," Brandon finished, coming back into the conversation. Suddenly he put his arms around Jessica and Elizabeth. He looked directly into Jessica's eyes. "I'll be happy to go over your lines with you two today," he offered.

"That would be wonderful, Brandon," Jessica said, her voice barely above a sigh.

Oh, brother! Elizabeth thought. *I may gag!*

"Well, I'll leave them in your capable hands, then," Marve said. "Feel free to grab a script, ask around for who's in the scene with you, and do some line reading today. We won't do the blocking and dress rehearsals until Sunday."

"Oh, I almost forgot," Natasha said. "Drop by wardrobe before you leave and get fitted for next week's outfits."

"We will," Elizabeth said. "And thanks for all of your help." She turned back to Jessica and Brandon, ready to run lines, but found them strolling off into the makeshift sunset.

Elizabeth clapped her hand over her mouth, stifling a giggle. *I hope I'm not the one who's supposed to get the guy*, she thought. *Because I don't want him!*

Nine

Despite all her fears, the Sunday rehearsal went well. By Monday morning, Elizabeth was ready for her first day of filming.

"If I just keep reminding myself that I'm here as a reporter on assignment, maybe I won't be so nervous," she whispered to Jessica as they walked down the hall to the makeup room.

"It's no big deal," Jessica told her. "You know your lines, right?"

"I went over them enough times this weekend," Elizabeth agreed, "but it's not the same as acting them out with ten cameras in your face."

"Relax. You'll be fine. And it's only three cameras," Jessica quipped, undaunted by the makeup woman slapping pancake on her face. "Besides, if you mess up, there are always retakes. It's not like being on Broadway, where the performances are live."

Elizabeth relaxed a little. She wished that she

and Jessica had spent more time practicing, but Brandon Hunter had monopolized most of Jessica's time over the weekend. Elizabeth couldn't help worrying about Sam. Where did he end up in all this?

"Did you call Sam at all this weekend, Jess?" Elizabeth finally asked.

"I didn't have a chance," Jessica replied as she checked her face in the mirror and then got up out of the chair so that Elizabeth could sit down.

"What's going on with you two? I haven't seen him around in ages."

"He's upset because I'm so busy, that's all," Jessica said lightly. "I'm sure we'll work things out when this is all over."

"I hope so," Elizabeth said seriously. She wanted to say more about how Sam was worth a thousand Brandon Hunters, but the makeup technician was right there, and besides, she didn't think Jessica would listen to anything negative about her hero.

A few minutes later, there was no more time to talk. The twins were out on the set, ready to begin their first scene.

"OK, twins," William announced over the loudspeaker from the control booth. "This is your first scene. Now, you know the story. Liz—now known as Tiffany—is a real schemer. She knows that Brandon, as Jeremy Howard, is leaning his affections toward Jess, now known as Heather—we'll call everyone by their stage names from now on. So in this scene, Tiffany is going to pretend to be Heather to try to trick Jeremy into noticing her. Got it?"

"Got it!" Elizabeth and Jessica said at once.

"Unh-unh, hang on," Brandon said. He shuffled through his script. "Why didn't someone tell me we were doing this scene first? I'm ready for the restaurant scene, not this one."

"Take five everybody," William said. "Brandon, get those lines down."

"It's not my fault that the whole taping schedule gets changed around for a couple of schoolkids."

"Brandon acts as if it's *our* fault that he doesn't know his lines," Elizabeth mentioned quietly to Jessica.

Stars in her eyes, Jessica replied. "Well, it must be tough. He's used to things going smoothly, and we're sort of throwing a glitch in the works."

"That's no excuse," Elizabeth said to an unhearing Jessica. "I thought he was supposed to be a professional!"

Throughout the morning, Brandon's behavior went from rude to obnoxious. Even Bruce Patman, Elizabeth thought, in all his egocentric glory, didn't come close to Brandon's conceit.

"Take three," Rick, the floor manager, called, slapping the clapboard in front of the camera.

Elizabeth glanced over at Jessica on the sidelines. Jessica smiled and gave her the thumbs-up sign for good luck.

"Action," William said.

" 'Oh, Jeremy,' " Elizabeth, as Tiffany, gushed, feigning surprise for the third time. " 'I didn't realize that you would be coming to the hospital today. I hope everything is fine with your mother.' "

" 'Why, Heather,' " Brandon, as Jeremy, crooned.

" 'I'm glad to see you. And yes, my father is fine.' "

"Cut!" William yelled. "That's *mother*, Jeremy," he told Brandon. "Your mother is having surgery, not your father."

"How am I supposed to remember from one minute to the next who's on their deathbed around here?" Brandon argued.

"Just take it from the top," William said.

Elizabeth rolled her eyes at Jessica, and Jessica grinned back.

"Take four," Rick said. *Snap!*

Elizabeth was in position. She started walking down the hospital corridor, looking for Brandon but trying not to appear as though she was. " 'Oh, Jeremy. I didn't realize that you would be coming into the hospital today,' " she said when she saw him. She adjusted her striped volunteer cap and schooled her face into a mask of concern. " 'I hope everything is fine with your mother.' "

" 'Why, Tiffany,' " Brandon crooned badly.

"Cut! You're supposed to think she's Heather," William said. "Take five. Brandon, let's talk."

"I'm not taking the blame for this!" Brandon shouted. "I can't help it if you stick these novices in the show and expect us to work around them. I'm going to my dressing room. I'll be back out when you've organized things out here."

What an immature, pompous, temperamental . . . Elizabeth didn't finish her thought. William came over to her.

"I'm sorry if I did something wrong," Elizabeth said.

"You're doing a wonderful job," William said. "I'm sorry you had to witness one of our star's little outbursts."

"This happens often?"

"Every day. But Elizabeth, I'm counting on you not to put our squabbles in print. We like to keep them to ourselves."

"Don't worry! I know what's appropriate to expose and what should be private. I'll even let you read the article to check for accuracy before I submit it."

William shook his head and glanced in the direction of Brandon's dressing room. "I wish some other people around here had as much consideration."

The morning dragged on. William's patience with Brandon's star-studded antics was seemingly limitless. Elizabeth wondered what kept him from firing him and finding a new heartthrob. She decided it probably had something to do with contracts and lawsuits.

They taped the same scene six times before Brandon got his lines right, but as far as Elizabeth was concerned, he still couldn't act his way out of a paper bag. His movements were wooden and his delivery was uninspiring. She wondered what the female viewers saw in him.

"What a morning!" Elizabeth sighed, slumping into the passenger seat of the Jeep as Jessica got ready to drive them back to Sweet Valley. "I thought Brandon would never get his lines straight."

"He must have just been having a bad day,"

Jessica said, brushing off her sister's observation. "I'm sure he's usually much more suave."

Or much more stupid, Elizabeth thought. It was hard to believe, but Jessica was actually defending him. Elizabeth had thought that seeing him in action would show Jessica the truth about her small-screen idol, but apparently Elizabeth was the only twin who noticed his shortcomings.

"I'm going out tonight," Jessica announced as she steered the Jeep through traffic to the freeway entrance.

"You and Sam? I'm glad to hear that. You've really been neglecting him lately."

"Not Sam," Jessica corrected her. "Brandon and I are going to dinner at Spago in Los Angeles. Isn't that exciting? All the stars eat there!"

"Have you even given a thought to Sam during all of this?" Elizabeth asked her. "A guy can only take so much, you know."

"He should have thought of that before he walked out on me the other day at the Dairi Burger," Jessica responded.

"He walked out on you?" Elizabeth exclaimed. "You didn't tell me that! You said he was just having a little trouble because you were so busy."

"Well, it was a little more than that," Jessica admitted. "He told me that he didn't think he'd ever understand me. See, I had to turn down a date with him to get my homework done. *Some* sacrifices have to be made, you know."

"You're not sacrificing your dates with Brandon," Elizabeth reminded her. "Maybe *that's* why Sam is so upset."

"My dates with Brandon are more like business," Jessica said as she took the freeway on-ramp and accelerated to cruising speed. "But I have to tell you, I could easily fall for Brandon Hunter!"

"You have to be kidding!" Elizabeth cried. "Sam is so much more . . . so much better than . . ."

"Yeah, but why should I hang around with someone who can't handle my fame?" Jessica asked. "Sam hasn't been the least bit supportive of me. Brandon, on the other hand, understands the spotlight, and the demands that an acting career makes on a person's social life."

Elizabeth couldn't think of a single word to reply to that silly statement, so she just stared at Jessica.

"Let's not fight," Jessica said, throwing her head back and letting her hair blow in the warm breeze as she drove. "Just think. This afternoon we get to watch ourselves on *The Young and the Beautiful* for the very first time! Let's invite everyone over for our premiere to celebrate."

"OK," Elizabeth agreed, laying her head back against the seat and closing her eyes. "As long as I have time to write up the first article before Wednesday at noon."

For the next two days the girls were caught up in their own personal whirlwind. Each morning they drove into Los Angeles at five o'clock to rehearse and film that day's scenes. The fast pace seemed to come naturally to Jessica, who scrambled to learn her lines just before each scene. Elizabeth, on the other hand, was beginning to feel the strain because of the extra time she was putting in on the articles for the *Los Angeles Times*.

"This is like having three full-time jobs," Elizabeth complained to Todd on Wednesday before their friends gathered in the Wakefield living room to watch the latest episode of *The Young and the Beautiful*. "I'm exhausted."

"You'll make it," Todd reassured her. "It's only two more days."

"It feels like two more years! I don't know how Jessica manages to look so perky all the time. Between the show, school, and trying to finish these articles for Rodney Grant at the *Times*, I must look like a worn-out dishrag."

"You look fine to me," Todd told her as he smoothed her hair back from her forehead and gave her a gentle kiss.

"Thanks for being patient with all this," Elizabeth said. "I really appreciate it."

"Actually, watching you on TV is kind of fun," he said. "For a week."

"Two more days. I'm glad it's almost over. Then maybe things can get back to normal around here."

The doorbell rang, and Jessica rushed from the kitchen to answer it, a bowl of popcorn in one hand.

"She's really into this, isn't she?" Todd remarked as their friends flowed into the room and Jessica began regaling them with the latest tidbits and hot gossip from the soap.

"She really is," Elizabeth said, watching the scene at the door from the comfort of the sofa. "I just wish Jessica would remember that when the week is over she's going to have to pick up all of the pieces of her old life. Poor Sam. He called Monday and Tuesday, but she hasn't even returned his calls. Instead, she went out with Brandon Hunter both nights. Boy, could I do an article on that guy!"

"Hey, how did it go today when you took your first article into the *Times*? Did you get to meet your editor?"

Elizabeth sat up, suddenly refreshed. "I haven't even had a chance to tell you. Not only did I get to meet him, but he took the time right then to read my article, and he said he really liked it. He's looking forward to getting the next two."

"That's great! When will the first one be published?"

"On Thursday—tomorrow. I can hardly wait! And now I'll be able to afford that new word processor I've been wanting. I have to give Jessica credit. This week may be hard, but it's helping us get two things we wanted—the Jeep *and* my new computer."

Todd squeezed her to him. "Trust you to find the positive side."

Ten

Jessica was in the middle of a juicy tale of intrigue concerning a future story line that she had overheard the producer talking about when the doorbell rang.

Elizabeth was on the couch talking softly with Todd and Enid. Jessica wanted the rest of her friends to finish watching her on TV, so she excused herself and jumped up to answer the door.

"Yes?" she said as she opened the door wide. "May I help you?"

Standing in front of her was a young man dressed as Batman, in full black and gold costume, including mask. He carried a bouquet of flowers in his hand, and he wore a solemn expression on his face.

Silently he handed her the flowers and a card, then waited while she read it.

" 'Dear Jessica,' " Jessica read aloud. " 'I miss you and want to speak with you as soon as possible. Will you please send a return message to let me know if I still mean anything to you? Love, Sam.' "

Jessica felt a sting of tears in her eyes as she read the note. It was true. She really hadn't paid much attention to Sam for the past week. She had been too busy with the show, school, and Brandon.

She wasn't really mad at Sam anymore, just hurt that he didn't understand how much being on *The Young and the Beautiful* meant to her. And he had gone to so much trouble to get in touch with her! The costumed messenger and the flowers were so romantic. Maybe he wanted to apologize.

The others had gathered around to see what was going on at the door. "From Sam," she said, waving the note in front of them. "Isn't he thoughtful?"

"I think the messenger is waiting for a reply," Enid observed.

Jessica turned back to the boy at the door. "Of course I'll see Sam," she told Batman. "Tell him that I'm free tonight."

At that Batman's stoic face broke into a wide grin. He let out a whoop and tore off his mask. It was Sam!

Jessica didn't even have time to react before he had grabbed her and bent her over backward for a passionate kiss.

After an instant of total shock, Jessica threw her arms around Sam's neck and played up the kiss to the enjoyment of all her fans.

Lila, Bruce, Amy, and the others all hooted and clapped for the clutching couple.

Elizabeth shook her head in mock dismay at Enid. "It's a disgrace," she said, trying not to laugh.

"I know," Enid said. "The people you hang around with, now that you're famous."

"I'd give that a ten!" Jessica said dramatically, when Sam finally let her up for air. "That was worth waiting for!"

Sam put his arms around her and mugged for their audience. "Did I miss the show?"

"I have it on tape," Jessica said. "All three episodes so far. Do you want to watch them now? Or shall we go for a drive in my new Jeep!"

"Catch everybody later," Sam said, twirling around with Jessica still in tow. "I want to have my girl alone for a while."

More hoots and catcalls followed them out the door.

"They're crazy," Jessica said, jerking a thumb back in the direction of the house.

"Sometimes I think I am, too," Sam said in a way that made Jessica wonder whether he was joking or not.

She flitted ahead and jumped into the driver's side of the Jeep.

Sam peeled off his costume to reveal denim shorts and a fluorescent green tank top underneath. The color really brought out the blond highlights in his hair and made him look even more tan than usual.

"Let's go to the beach!" Jessica suggested as she

backed out of the garage and headed down the street.

"Anywhere is fine with me, as long as we can talk."

Though Jessica was glad to be with Sam, she found that she didn't want to talk about anything but the show. She showered him with the same stories she had been telling everyone else all week—after all, Sam hadn't been there the first few times she had told them—as she drove to a secluded, semiprivate beach out on Route 1.

They parted and got out of the car, then walked hand in hand down to the water's edge.

Dimly, Jessica realized that she was checking around for reporters when they parked. She had become accustomed to the media trailing her and Brandon around, snapping pictures. She didn't really want a photographer sneaking up on her now, when she was with Sam. She wondered how Brandon would take it if he saw a picture of her and Sam in the paper.

For the first time she wondered whether Brandon would be hurt if he knew she had a boyfriend. She had sort of conveniently not mentioned this fact to him on any of their many dates. Brandon was really a nice guy, despite what Elizabeth thought, and she didn't want to hurt him if he actually was falling in love with her.

Of course, she didn't really think he was. He was probably only being nice during her week of working on the show. On the other hand, Jessica wasn't really sure what *she* was feeling for Brandon. She liked him—he was charming and debonair, oh-so-suave—and she loved the fancy parties, limousine rides, and expensive dinners. But did she *love* Brandon? Was it possible to love two guys at once?

She decided that she didn't want to think about her love dilemma. When she was with Brandon, she would pay attention to Brandon. Right now she was with Sam, and she would pay attention to him.

"Did I tell you what happened this morning when I was bending over to pick up a piece of paper on the set?" she said, breaking the silence that had reigned since they had left the Jeep. "Well, the outfit that they had me in was so tight that—"

"Jessica," Sam interjected, "why haven't you returned my phone calls lately? What's going on with you and this Hunter guy? I don't really like what I'm reading in the papers."

"There's nothing to worry about," Jessica said, taking off her sandals and skipping down to dip her toes in the foamy surf.

"I'm not blind. I've seen the way that guy is looking at you in those photographs. *And* the way you're looking at him," Sam accused. "I know that you've been going out with him almost every night. I'd like to know who you think your boyfriend is?"

"I'm not going out with him tonight," Jessica said, trying to ignore the tone in Sam's voice. "Tonight I'm out with you, walking along a romantic beach, waiting for the sunset." She turned into his arms and kissed him. "Does that answer your question?"

111

"No!" Sam said. "You kiss me as if nothing has changed, but everything *has* changed. I don't like playing second fiddle to a second-rate actor. And besides, everyone thinks you're having an affair with him."

"An affair?" Jessica scoffed. "That's simply not true. All our dates have been very innocent."

"Maybe on your part, Jess," Sam said. "But the gossip columnists are having a field day. I read an article just today about Jessica Wakefield's tips for holding on to an older man. There were a bunch of quotes from you that didn't sound very innocent to me."

"Well, they were all made up. I haven't told any reporters stuff like that. It's just harmless publicity."

Sam stopped walking and took a stance, his back to the setting sun. "A little publicity is one thing. I can handle a little publicity. But I don't like being made to look like a fool!"

"No one is making you look like a fool," Jessica said, wondering how to turn this conversation around. Humor might work, she thought. "Speaking of fools, did I tell you what happened the other day on the set when the cameraman accidentally forgot to put the film in the camera? We shot seven scenes and had to do them all over again. . . ."

"Your stories don't impress me, Jessica," Sam said. "You're so starstruck that you don't even realize what I'm saying."

"Of course I know what you're saying. But I don't want to have a serious talk right now. I've been working hard all day. I want to relax and enjoy the sunset."

"OK," Sam agreed reluctantly. "As long as we promise to talk later." They sat down on the sand, their legs extended so that the water just lapped at their bare toes.

Jessica was glad not to have to talk about her relationship with Brandon for a while, but she couldn't help thinking about it. She just wasn't sure how she felt about him, and she certainly couldn't explain her mixed feelings to Sam at the moment. To be honest, she was just kind of biding her time until the week was over, until she saw what happened. She figured that the show *and* her relationship with Brandon would both come to an end at that time, but on the other hand . . . maybe it *would* be interesting to keep dating him after their parts on the show were over. But then what would she do about Sam? Oh, she didn't want to lose him, either!

It was too much to think about. "The sunset is beautiful," Jessica said, forcing her thoughts away from the two men in her life.

"I'm glad we came," Sam murmured softly as he put his arm around her.

They sat quietly for a few moments, absorbing the solitude of the evening, but Jessica was still too excited about her day to sit still for long. She just *had* to tell Sam all the great things that had been happening to her.

"The director says I should have a portfolio of headshots taken to send out to agents," Jessica said. She moved away from him a little and struck

113

a pose, letting the fading sun's last warm rays touch her hair and burnish it a beautiful golden color.

"Do you think using the sunset as a background would be a good idea?" she asked.

Sam stared at her, openmouthed. When he finally spoke, his voice was low, almost too quiet for her to hear. "I'm tired of the glitz and the glamour, Jessica. You've gone off on some crazy tangents in the past, but this one is the craziest. I don't even know you anymore!"

Jessica stared back at Sam. She just couldn't understand his attitude at all. Here she was, trying to include him in her life, trying to tell him about the possibilities for her future, and all he wanted to talk about was how crazy she was.

Suddenly the uncertainty, tension, and excitement of the past week came crashing in on her. Maybe Sam had a right to be a little jealous, but Jessica did not think she deserved *this* attitude. She was not just playing a game. Her career meant a lot to her.

"You want to talk? Let's talk! If you ask me," Jessica said, her voice rising, "*you're* the one who's overreacting!"

"I may be," Sam countered, "but I'm not going to follow you around like a puppy dog, waiting for you to toss a few tidbits my way. I think you need to make a choice, Jessica. It's either Brandon Hunter or me!"

By this time, Jessica was mad. Really mad. She didn't like demands, from Sam or from anyone else. She was her own boss, and no one, boyfriend or not, was going to give her ultimatums.

"Well?" Sam prompted. "Who is it going to be?"

"Fine!" Jessica shouted. "You made the choice for me with your demands and accusations. I have more important things to do than soothe the overinflated ego of a high school boy!"

With that parting shot, Jessica got up and stomped off to the Jeep, leaving Sam stranded.

She *did* have important things to do, she told herself as she drove off in a cloud of dust and flying sand. There were lines to memorize and a date with Brandon the next night at an awards banquet. She saw her future clearly laid out in front of her—and if Sam didn't want to try to fit into it, that was his choice!

Eleven

"I think I'm actually beginning to enjoy this a little," Elizabeth told Jessica on Thursday morning, when they were rehearsing their second-to-last scene.

"I think you just like arguing with me," Jessica teased.

"Well, it *is* kind of fun pretending to be snobby and self-centered and . . ."

"Downright vicious?" Jessica supplied.

"Thank you." Elizabeth laughed. "Are you ready, *Heather*? This is going to be our first—and last—scene with only us on the screen. The Wakefields take TV-land."

"I'm as ready as I'll ever be, *Tiffany*."

"Scene three, take one," Rick called, followed by the familiar snap of the clapboard.

Instantly, Jessica and Elizabeth were in character.

" 'There you are,' " Elizabeth accused as she

116

came through the door onto the set from backstage. " 'It's just like you, Heather, to disappear when something important needs to be discussed.' "

" 'I didn't disappear,' " Jessica said meekly. " 'I was in the library reading.' "

" 'Reading, reading!' " Elizabeth scoffed. " 'That's a good excuse! I know you were in here plotting to steal Jeremy Howard away from me. You just can't stand it that he prefers someone with a little life in her to a quiet little mouse like you!' "

" 'I'm sure that Jeremy can make up his own mind.' " Jessica sighed. " 'Of course,' " she asserted mildly, " 'it *would* help if you weren't always trying to confuse him by pretending to be me.' "

" 'Me?' " Elizabeth shouted. " 'How dare you accuse me of underhanded tactics? You're the one who always manages to be at his mother's bedside, acting like a goody-two-shoes every time he goes to visit her.' "

" 'I don't plan that,' " Jessica said.

" 'Oh, and I suppose that getting a job in the store where he frequently shops was an accident also?' "

" 'Yes, it was.' "

" 'Well, I don't believe it! Tomorrow night at the party, everyone will know that Jeremy Howard is mine! I'll bet he doesn't even give you the time of day!' "

Jessica's smile was sweet and placid. " 'I think, sister dear, that for all your bravado, you're scared. You're frightened to death that

Jeremy might have seen through your ploys and will drop you tomorrow night in front of all of our friends.' "

Elizabeth stomped to the window, threw open the curtain, and stared out. " 'I'm afraid of no such thing!' "

" 'We'll see,' " Jessica said, bending her head once again over her book.

The cameraman signaled that he had faded out the scene, and Jessica and Elizabeth relaxed.

"Cut! That's a wrap," William said.

"We don't have to do it again?" Jessica asked.

"Nope. It was just fine the first time."

Because Brandon wasn't in it, Elizabeth concluded, but she didn't voice her thoughts aloud. It was obvious to her that Jessica liked him an awful lot, even though everyone else on the set barely seemed to tolerate his presence.

William continued, "Nice cliff-hanger, girls. Are you ready for the big party scene tomorrow?"

"I feel as if this whole week has been a party!" Jessica exuded. "I've had so much fun!"

"How about you, Liz?" William turned to her and asked. "Although you've been doing a wonderful job on camera, you're not as thrilled as Jess to be on the show, are you?"

"That shows, does it?" Elizabeth said ruefully. "I have to admit that at the beginning I was skeptical, maybe even a trifle smug. I thought soap opera actors were overpaid and underworked, and I really didn't see the appeal of watching a bunch of people dig themselves into one problem situation after another."

118

"Liz!" Jessica tried to hush her.

"It's all right," William said, his eyes twinkling. "I appreciate her honesty. How do you feel now?"

"Now I realize how hard everyone works to put out a good product. I plan to talk about both the glamour *and* the hard-work aspects in my last article. And I really appreciate the cast and crew being so open and helpful with me. The editor at the *L.A. Times* is very pleased with my articles and with the black and white photos I've submitted showing life on a soap set."

"He thinks it really gives the readers the added dimension that's been missing in the past from stories like these," Jessica added, obviously very proud of her sister's accomplishments.

Elizabeth smiled self-consciously.

"I'm glad you've had a change of heart," William added. "And I'm glad you're tearing away some of the veils and explaining terms like *gaffer* and *grip* that tend to confuse TV viewers."

"You've read the first article? In this morning's edition?" Elizabeth exclaimed.

"Of course," William said. "Even though you showed me the article before you gave it to your editor, but you never know what might happen before a story like that gets into print. I must say, though, you've been more than fair. Most writers tear us apart looking for the dirt. And there's plenty of dirt here," he added, waving his arm around.

"That doesn't really serve any purpose, does it?" Elizabeth said. "I just thought people should know about what *really* goes on. It's dramatic enough without adding fuel to the gossip fire."

"Between you and me," William said, leaning closer, "don't get too caught up in the drama. Soap operas are still mostly fluff. We're trying to entertain people, not solve the world's problems."

Elizabeth smiled as he walked off. "I really like him," she told Jessica. "It's too bad I won't be doing another article so that I could profile him in depth. I think he's the backbone of the whole show. But tomorrow will be our last day on the set, and I'll be turning in my last article on Monday."

"Last show, last article." Jessica sighed. "I wish it didn't all have to end."

"It may not have to," Natasha said, coming up to them. "You two have done such a nice job this week that there may be further work on *The Young and the Beautiful* for you. After all, we can't give Jeremy a girlfriend and then have her disappear out of his life, now can we?"

"I . . . guess not," Jessica stammered. "But our contracts say only one week's worth of episodes."

"True," she said, as she headed off after William. Then she called back over her shoulder, "But we can always negotiate new contracts."

For once in her life Jessica was speechless.

"Close your mouth, Jess," Elizabeth said with a laugh. "Didn't you even suspect that the parts of Heather and Tiffany might go on after this week?"

"No! Well, I hoped . . . well, I wished . . ." Suddenly she found her voice. "Liz, this is the break I've been waiting for. This could launch me into show business!" Then another thought hit her. "It will be so much easier for Brandon and I to keep seeing each other. We'll be equals. . . ."

"Slow down, Jess. It hasn't happened yet, and it might not. Natasha was just speculating. If I were you, I wouldn't get your hopes up about the show *or* about Brandon."

"I can't help it. I want to be an actress, and Brandon Hunter is going to be standing right beside me in my climb to the top!"

Elizabeth put her hand on Jessica's shoulder. "I thought you were only seeing Brandon for this week, and then you were going to start paying more attention to Sam."

A frown creased Jessica's forehead. "I'm not sure that Sam wants to have anything to do with me if I pursue a career in acting. I didn't tell you this, but you know when we drove off to the beach last night?"

"Yes?"

"Well, we had a fight, and I sort of drove off and left him stranded."

"You what?" Elizabeth hissed. "Oh, Jessica! That's awful!"

Jessica sighed. "I know. But Sam said some really cruel things to me. He told me I was making a fool of him by going out with Brandon and that I would have to make a choice between them."

"I'm almost afraid to ask what happened next," Elizabeth said.

"I got mad and chose Brandon."

"You didn't!"

"What else was I supposed to do? Sam was

making all these demands and accusations. It serves him right!" Jessica declared. "I'm my own person. I run my own life! At least Brandon has appreciated my talent and drive this week. Who knows? Maybe something more can develop between us. I *do* like him, and I know he likes me."

"I hope you know what you're doing," Elizabeth said as she looked at her watch. There was no sense trying to reason with Jessica when she was off on one of her fame-and-fortune flings. Maybe they could talk more on the way home. "Right now, we'd better get these clothes and our makeup off and climb into the Jeep for the ride back to Sweet Valley. I have a history test this afternoon and a noon deadline to beat tomorrow."

"I'll meet you in our dressing room in a few minutes. I want to stop by Brandon's dressing room and tell him the good news about us possibly being on the show longer."

"But you're going to see him tonight at the awards banquet," Elizabeth reminded her.

"I can't wait that long," Jessica said as she ran off in the opposite direction.

Jessica skipped down the corridor to Brandon's dressing room. *He's going to be so excited*, she told herself. *We'll be able to stay together*. She tried not to think about Sam. Maybe if she threw herself completely into her new life, it wouldn't hurt so much that Sam wasn't going to be in it.

She reached Brandon's door and did a quick, jubilant pirouette. Hand on the doorknob, she was about to burst in with her good news when she heard her name mentioned, followed by the words "great idea," then by Brandon's familiar laugh.

Her hand dropped down to her side as she listened. Maybe they were planning to give her a part in Brandon's new movie? She put her ear closer to the door.

Jessica recognized Marve's voice. "Yep, this publicity stunt was the best one you've dreamed up yet."

"As soon as I saw her, I knew she would fall for it," Brandon said, still chuckling. "She's such a naive and quiet little thing, just like her character."

Jessica's smile dropped off of her face, and her hands clenched.

"She really believes that you fell for her!" Marve continued. "And so did all the papers. Our ratings have soared this week because the fans think there's romance both on and off the screen for their favorite hunk."

"Shall I flex a muscle?" Brandon joked.

"Only if there's a photographer present," Marve remarked.

"Did you see some of those mug shots I took with her?"

Mug shots?

"You looked like the picture of blossoming young love."

"Young is right," Brandon scoffed. "I'll be glad when this week is over, and she heads back to high school. I need a little more sophistication in my life. I think I'll start pursuing Sandi Starr.

Now, there's a woman who would be good for my career!"

Marve let out a low whistle. "The daughter of the studio's owner? You sure know how to stack your deck."

Jessica didn't wait around to hear more. She ran down the hall, tears in her eyes. She was about to burst in on Elizabeth and tell her everything she had heard—how Brandon's whirlwind courtship with her had all been a scam, a carefully staged performance to improve the ratings.

Then she stopped and took a deep breath. *Could she be jumping to conclusions?* They couldn't have been talking about her, could they? No, she decided, calming down. After the first mention of her name and the words "great idea," they had never said her name again.

"They must have been referring to someone else—maybe a new story line that they're working on," she whispered to the empty corridor.

On the other hand, wasn't she kind of doing the same thing to Brandon—using him to further her career? But she *had* thought he genuinely liked her! And someone who liked her wouldn't be that calculating and underhanded—especially not her loving, attentive, handsome Brandon. Would he?

Twelve

By the time Jessica had taken off her makeup, she
was composed. There was no reason to tell her
suspicions to Elizabeth. Elizabeth couldn't stand
Brandon, and this would just give her more
ammunition.

Still, Jessica was willing to give Brandon the
benefit of the doubt until that evening. During
the awards banquet she would watch him very
carefully and objectively. Then she would decide
what to do. It was one thing if two people who
liked and respected each other helped each other
out with their mutual careers. That was what Jessica had *thought* she and Brandon were doing. But
it was quite another thing if all of the liking and
respecting were on one side only.

Because of all the thoughts racing around inside
her head, Jessica was quiet on the way home and
grateful that Elizabeth didn't ask about Brandon's
reaction to her news.

What if I've really blown it? Jessica thought now. She had dropped Sam, hoping Brandon would be there to take his place, and then she had discovered that Brandon was a jerk. Well, he *might* be a jerk. And if he was, then *she* would end up being the loser. Jessica didn't like that idea very much. She also didn't like thinking that maybe Sam and Elizabeth had been right about her all along—that she had been self-centered and so totally caught up in the acting thing that she had forgotten what was real and important in her life—her family and her friends.

"We've barely had a chance to talk since the beginning of the week," Mrs. Wakefield said as they sat down to dinner that evening. She smiled around the table at Jessica, Elizabeth, Steven, and their father. "It's nice to have all our children home for a change."

"Somehow I think evenings like this are only going to become more scarce as time goes on," Mr. Wakefield said. "I see more of Jessica in the tabloids than I do at home lately," he teased.

"I'm sorry about some of those stories," Jessica said quickly. "I hope you know that most of what they say is made up."

"It's a good thing!" Mrs. Wakefield said. "People are starting to talk. Luckily, no one that matters believes a word of those stories."

"Why, what are people saying?" Jessica asked.

"Well, all the guys at college are hounding me to introduce them to you two," Steven said.

"They think you're . . . um . . . hot, after what they've seen on TV and read in the papers."

"Is that good or bad?" Jessica remarked, looking at Elizabeth.

"I'm not sure," Steven said. "I find myself defending your honor a lot lately."

"Thanks," Elizabeth said. "But as Mom mentioned, the people who *matter* don't believe the lies."

"Yeah, thanks," Jessica said. "I appreciate that." She was beginning to wonder just *what* all the crazy publicity was really doing to her reputation. At one time she had been hung up on dating college guys, but since she and Sam had started going together, that particular qualification hadn't mattered to her. Now it seemed college guys were interested in her only because of her new "image."

And come to think of it, the guys at school had been hovering around her more than usual this week, too, even asking for dates. Sam had said the articles made him feel like a fool. Maybe *she* was the only one foolish enough to think that lies told about her in the press didn't mean anything.

"Oh, by the way, your math teacher called me at work today," Mr. Wakefield said, breaking into Jessica's troubled thoughts.

"Uh-oh," Jessica murmured, dragging herself back into the conversation. "I failed the math test, didn't I?"

"She's concerned that you're a bit overextended, that's all," Mr. Wakefield said.

"Look, everybody," Jessica said. "I know things

have been a little crazy around here for the past week, and I know I've been caught up in the whirlwind of it all. I promise things will get back to normal soon."

"How about you, Elizabeth?" Steven asked. "Are you caught up in all this craziness, too?"

"Not the same way that Jess is," Elizabeth replied. "But all the commuting, extra studying, and trying to beat the deadlines for the articles in the *Times* is beginning to get to me. I'll be glad when things return to normal, too. It's been fun, though. I'm glad we did it."

"Me, too," Jessica agreed. "I've learned a lot." *Unfortunately, the lessons were even harder to learn than math*, she added silently.

"You look beautiful," Brandon told her when the limousine deposited her at the entrance to the convention center where the awards banquet was to take place. "Thanks for understanding about my not being able to pick you up."

"Oh, I understand," Jessica said sweetly, turning on all her charm but making a mental note of how many times Brandon had sent someone else to pick her up instead of coming himself.

A few minutes later, Jessica, decked out more extravagantly than usual in a floor-length royal purple chiffon-and-lace gown, and Brandon, in one of his five-thousand-dollar tuxedos, stepped onto the red carpet leading to the entrance.

Photographers were stationed all along the route, and Jessica smiled until she thought her lips would stick to her teeth. Brandon stopped several times to give a particular reporter a better shot, and each time, he put his arm possessively around Jessica's shoulders or waist. One time he even leaned in for a chaste kiss on her cheek as the flashbulbs popped.

Hypocrite, Jessica thought angrily. *He never acts loving when we're alone. In fact, come to think of it, I'm usually left alone when we go somewhere, while Brandon runs around conducting business.*

Jessica's eyes narrowed as they took their seats, and Brandon immediately leaned over and engaged the person on his other side in conversation.

Why didn't I see the truth before? He isn't even remotely paying attention to me!

"Brandon, dear," Jessica gushed, interrupting his conversation. "I think this nice man over here wants to take our picture."

Brandon immediately became attentive, and it was all Jessica could do not to stick her tongue out at the last second before the photographer pushed the shutter button.

"Will you excuse me for a moment?" Brandon asked her when the photographer had moved off. "I see someone on the other side of the room that I have to speak to."

You jerk! Trying to abandon me again, aren't you?

"Why, you know," Jessica cooed, "after that long limousine ride, I could use a little exercise. Why don't I walk over there with you and you can introduce me?"

Brandon's carefully constructed mask of sincerity slipped for just a second. "Uh, now that I think about it," he finally said, "the program is almost ready to begin. We can socialize later."

Creep! You didn't expect me to be assertive, did you? Jessica thought. *You think I really am Heather, the demure one, don't you?*

"You know, Brandon," Jessica continued, "I enjoy meeting all your friends. And now that I may be on the show permanently, I hope to meet so many more of them," Jessica told him sweetly.

"Permanently?" he exclaimed.

Jessica smiled, enjoying his discomfort. "Yes, Natasha told me today that the producers are thinking seriously of continuing my role after the week is out."

Jessica wanted Brandon to squirm. Even though he had managed to compose himself and slap his smiling mask back on his face, she knew he wasn't at all happy with her at that moment. Had she been *so* gullible before that she had mistaken the insincere tone in his voice, the false look of adoration in his eyes for *love*?

As the awards banquet and ceremony wore on, Jessica became increasingly aware of Brandon's obnoxious personality.

"Did you know that I'm up for three awards tonight, Jessie?" Brandon told her proudly. "You may have to help me carry them all out. Wouldn't that be a good picture for the front page of tomorrow's paper?"

"I'll be happy to help you carry them out," Jessica said, trying to curb the sarcasm in her voice. She batted her eyelashes and added innocently, "It will be almost like winning them *myself!*"

"I knew you'd feel that way. You understand me so well," Brandon commented.

What a conceited . . . rotten . . . ! Elizabeth had been right all along. Every word out of his mouth was fake. *I actually broke up with Sam over him!* Jessica winced.

Well, if her relationship with Brandon was all an elaborate ploy to raise the ratings, then her performance as his doting new girlfriend that evening deserved an Academy Award.

". . . and I just spent four hundred thousand dollars on a new Arabian stallion to breed with my mares. . . . Are you listening to me, Jessica?" Brandon was asking.

"Of course I'm listening," Jessica said. "I've truly enjoyed hearing about your prize Arabian stallions and your Russian wolfhounds. Tell me again how you broke your first wild bronco when you were eight years old. I never get tired of that story!"

Brandon completely missed the sarcastic tone of Jessica's words and launched into his embellished account of capturing a wild horse and taming it to obey his every command while Jessica gazed at him with mock adoring eyes. *Funny, this story is beginning to sound a lot like "The Black Stallion,"* she thought. She was beginning to wonder about his hang gliding and championship waterskiing episodes, too.

I'll bet every story he's told me has been lifted from a book or TV show. The real Brandon Hunter is about as courageous as a baby chick!

"I enjoy riding, too," Jessica said when he took a breath. "Maybe we could go riding sometime up at the stables in Sweet Valley. There's nothing like galloping on the beach at dawn."

"Yes, well, uh . . . did I tell you about the time I single-handedly wrestled an alligator to save my co-star in one of the movies I was doing?"

"No, Brandon. I haven't heard that story," Jessica said. *Hmm*, Jessica thought, *so Brandon saw "Crocodile Dundee," did he?* "You actually wrestled an alligator? Weren't you scared?"

Brandon fell easily into another too-good-to-be-true tale of derring-do as Jessica silently plotted her revenge.

You made a fool out of me, Brandon Hunter, she fumed silently. *No one, not even a big, famous soap opera star gets away with doing that to Jessica Wakefield. By tomorrow afternoon, I'll have found a way to get back at you. I promise!*

Then she smiled and leaned her chin in her hand, seemingly absorbed in his story.

Jessica's anger kept her face from falling apart until she walked in the door on Calico Drive late that night.

"How were the awards? We saw you on TV," her mother said.

"Fine," Jessica reported, swallowing the catch in her throat.

"Are you feeling all right, Jessica?" her father asked. "I don't suppose you're looking forward to tomorrow's final episode. Kind of a letdown, huh?"

"Actually, as I told you earlier, I'm kind of tired of the pace," Jessica said, pulling off her earrings and bending down to kiss both her parents goodnight. "I think I'll be happy when it's over."

She trudged up to her bedroom, the sting of tears causing her to blink. Elizabeth was just coming out of the bathroom as Jessica reached the top of the stairs.

"Jess, what's wrong?" Elizabeth asked immediately. "You look awful."

"Thanks," Jessica sniffed, one lone tear brimming over the inside corner of her left eye.

"You know I didn't mean it that way. Come into my room and tell me what happened. And don't try to say 'nothing,' because I'm your sister, and I can tell when you're upset!"

Before she reached Elizabeth's neatly made bed, Jessica was crying for real. "It's awful, Liz," she sobbed. "Brandon has been using me all week to get publicity for the show. All our dates, all those pictures in the papers, were fakes. *He's* a fake!"

"How did you find this out?" Elizabeth asked quietly.

"I overheard Brandon and Marve talking in Brandon's dressing room this morning. Marve was congratulating him on making a fool of me all week, and Brandon was planning who he was going to choose as his next victim."

"That *is* awful!" Elizabeth said, putting her arms around her twin and pulling her head down on her shoulder. "I knew that guy was a jerk, but I did think he cared about you a *little*."

"Not even a tiny bit," Jessica admitted. "I can't believe how smooth he was, or how stupid I was. I bought all his lines, all his false interest. But tonight I watched him, really listened to him for the first time."

"And . . . ?"

"And he's a liar and a cheat, and not a very good one at that. He's the most conceited, selfish snob I've ever met, and I'm going to get back at him if it's the last thing I do."

Elizabeth handed Jessica a tissue and sat back while she blew her nose. "Well, you used him a little, too," she reminded Jessica. "Remember that you wanted the attention from the media and from your friends. I'd say you both got *something* out of your week's fling with fame."

"Maybe," Jessica said with a hiccup. "But in the end, he wins—he gets better ratings and lots of publicity. He'll probably even sell some sob story to the press about how terrible I am. What do I get? I go back to school and lose all the contacts I made, and to top it all off, I don't even have a boyfriend to go back to. I'm miserable!" she wailed.

"C'mon, Jess," Elizabeth said. "It's true that what Brandon did was pretty slimy, and that things might look bad right now, but it's *not* the end of the world!"

"Liz, will you help me think of a way to get revenge before he has a chance to drop me publicly? I want to do something that puts a little chink in his self-image."

Jessica raised her tear-stained face to Elizabeth's and waited.

"That the spirit!" Elizabeth said. "I've been taking his garbage all week, too, and I think it's time Brandon Hunter figured out that there are more important things in life than a fat paycheck and a pretty face."

Jessica stood, smiling. "By the time we're finished, he'll be sorry he ever crossed the Wakefield twins!"

Elizabeth stood too and hugged Jessica. "I'm sorry today was so rotten for you," she said.

"Me, too. But tomorrow will be better!"

Jessica circled Elizabeth's room, trailing a finger along the cream-colored walls. "But what am I going to do about Sam? He'll never forgive me. And the worst part is that I've finally realized what a mistake I made by choosing Brandon over Sam. I still love him, Liz. I don't know. I guess my head was turned by all the glamour. And then, I really *did* think I was falling in love with Brandon."

Elizabeth sat down in her desk chair. "Everybody thinks about going out with someone else once in a while. Whenever Todd and my relationship begins to feel boring, it's easy to be tempted by other guys. But it doesn't take me long to realize that I want to work things out with Todd. Maybe this experience with Brandon has been a *good* thing, and maybe it will help your relationship with Sam grow."

"If he ever speaks to me again," Jessica said.

Elizabeth laughed. "By now, Sam, of all people, is used to your special brand of craziness. Hopefully he'll be understanding one more time."

"I know what I'll do," Jessica said. "As soon as the final taping is over tomorrow, and as soon as school lets out, I'll go to Sam's house and apologize, even if it means I have to shine up that bike of his to show him how much I care."

"Sounds like you're on the right track," Elizabeth said. "Now, what are we going to do to put Mr. Hunter in his place tomorrow?"

"How about this?" Jessica suggested. "We both know that Brandon is a bad actor. . . ."

"You knew that, too?" Elizabeth laughed. "I didn't think you had noticed."

"Here's my plan. We keep him off balance—not enough that anyone else would notice, but just enough to confuse him a little and make him flub his lines more than usual."

"So that they'll have to do a million takes?" Elizabeth asked, rubbing her hands together and grinning.

"There are a couple of places in our scenes where we could change clothes," Jessica suggested. "Or—you know that necklace I'm always supposed to wear so that Brandon can tell us apart and look intelligent onstage? Well, what if you wore it instead of me . . . ?"

"That's perfect. And I'll bet we could get Harold in special effects to make it snow a little when Brandon is looking out the window at the party."

"Snow in Southern California! I love it," Jessica said. "And hey, here's an idea. Let's sneak down to wardrobe and get rid of all of his ties except for that really wild one with the fish on it!"

Elizabeth giggled. "Wait a second. We're going to forget all these fabulous ideas. Let me take notes!"

Thirteen

"This is the big party scene, the climax for the week," William announced the next morning from his usual place in the control booth. "Take your chalk marks, everyone. Is everybody in position? Remember, this is where Jeremy makes his choice and he and Heather begin their happily-ever-after."

"Fat chance of that," Jessica muttered to Elizabeth. "Brandon had the nerve to kiss me good luck this morning! It took every ounce of willpower I had to keep from punching him in the nose."

"Don't get mad now—" Elizabeth began.

"I know—get even! Is Harold ready with the snow?" Jessica asked. "I've already asked Elaine from props to dress up in an outfit like mine to give Brandon a little double-vision."

Elizabeth nodded as Rick's clapboard snapped for the first take of the day. They both looked over at William, waiting for his signal. "Let's do it," she whispered.

Jessica gave her the thumbs-up sign.

"Action!" William called.

" 'I've been waiting for you,' " Elizabeth purred into Brandon's ear. " 'Isn't it a beautiful day? Why don't you walk with me to the window?' "

" 'Where's Heather?' " Brandon asked, glancing around.

Jessica's cue to appear within Brandon's view was not supposed to be until a few minutes later, but now she stepped casually out of the wings. Brandon could see her, although she wasn't on camera.

" 'She'll be along,' " Elizabeth said, making sure he saw Jessica in the wings. Then she turned him around and practically dragged him to the window. " 'I was hoping to speak with you alone for a moment.' "

" 'Uh, sure . . .' " he stammered, confused by the appearance of Jessica on the wrong side of the stage and too early.

"Cut!" William yelled over the loudspeaker. "What's the matter, Brandon?"

"Jessica is on the wrong side to enter on cue." He pointed an accusing finger to where Jessica had been standing, but Elaine was there instead, wearing the clothes just like those Jessica had been wearing.

"I'm over here, Brandon," Jessica twittered, stepping out from the right spot on the opposite side of the stage as if she had been there all along, when actually she had made a mad dash behind the sets the minute Brandon had looked away.

Brandon shook his head and turned back to re-take the scene. Meanwhile, Jessica ran back to the dressing room to change clothes. Her new outfit would be identical to Elizabeth's except that she would be wearing the choker necklace.

Jessica made it back to the set in time to enter on cue and see Brandon falling apart because of the snow Harold was spilling over what was supposed to be a sunny beach.

"Cut!" William said. "Problem?"

"It's snowing," Brandon said. "Special effects is messing up again. I told you that Harold couldn't do his job worth beans."

"I resent that!" Harold shouted from backstage.

"Rewind the tape," William instructed the woman operating the video monitor. "No snow here," he said, examining the scene as it played back.

Jessica smiled covertly at Elizabeth. Of course not. Harold was doing it only for Brandon's benefit, not enough to ruin the shot. The snow wasn't in the picture.

"Action!" William called again.

" 'Heather!' " Brandon greeted Jessica, glancing down at the ID necklace that she was wearing. " 'Tiffany and I were just talking about you. I'm so glad you were able to come.' "

In a minute you'll wish I hadn't, Jessica thought, holding out her hand to him. " 'I've missed you, Jeremy. I hope your mother is doing well.' "

" 'Yes, she'll be discharged from the hospital tomorrow morning.' "

Elizabeth-as-Tiffany glared at Jessica-as-Heather behind Brandon-as-Jeremy's back, apparently upset

139

that he had transferred his attention to her twin the minute she walked into the party.

" 'Jeremy!' " Elizabeth said forcefully. " 'What was that you were saying about raising funds for a new hospital wing at Seaside General? I'm sure I could use my considerable influence with the Board of Newtronics to convince them to contribute to such a worthy cause.' "

The camera focused on Brandon as he gazed off into space, apparently trying to decide what to say to Elizabeth. Jessica quickly handed Elizabeth the necklace behind his back and off camera.

Jessica touched Brandon's arm softly. "I'm feeling a little dizzy. I think I had better sit down." She swooned against him as the script dictated, and he gallantly assisted her to the sofa.

While Brandon was hovering over Jessica, Elizabeth slipped on the necklace. The script told Brandon to go get a drink of water for Jessica, but when he turned back with the water, the girl lying on the sofa didn't have the necklace. Elizabeth had taken the opportunity to sit down on the second sofa.

Camera still rolling, Brandon confidently strolled over to Elizabeth and handed her the water. " 'I've been meaning to talk with you, Heather,' " he said.

"Cut!"

"What now?" Brandon demanded.

"Wrong girl," William said, walking out on the set to speak with him.

While they were talking, Elizabeth and Jessica switched the necklace again.

Brandon turned back to yell at them for moving

around on the set but found everything as it should be. He was furious.

"I don't know what's going on here, but I'm being played for a fool!" he shouted.

Jessica opened her eyes innocently. "We wouldn't dream of treating you like that, Brandon," she said. "Maybe all those late nights are taking their toll. You probably just need a rest."

His eyes narrowed as he took in her sweet smile and guileless blue-green gaze.

Brandon stomped back to his position on the set and shouted for makeup to powder the sweat off his nose.

Jessica winked at Elizabeth. Their plan was working. By the time they had finished shooting all the scenes, it was late in the morning.

"Conference, everyone," William called. "Jessica, Elizabeth, I want to see you front and center!" he added.

"Uh-oh," Elizabeth said.

Jessica stood next to her and watched William come down out of the control booth. "Think he'll yell at us?" she whispered as the rest of the cast gathered around, too.

"I wouldn't be surprised," Elizabeth whispered back.

But when William reached them, he was smiling. "I just wanted to say goodbye," he told them. "I think I speak for the entire cast and crew when I say that we've really enjoyed working with you two this week."

Jessica and Elizabeth breathed twin sighs of relief. "We've really enjoyed working with you all, too," Elizabeth said.

"I hope you'll feel that you can come back to the set and visit anytime," Natasha added. "And who knows. You may be back sooner than you think."

"That would be great!" Jessica said. "I'm sorry everything took so long this morning." She really *was* sorry—for William's sake, not for Brandon's.

William cast a disparaging glance in Brandon's direction. "I'm sure it won't be the last time," he commented.

The rest of the cast and the crew gathered around to say their own goodbyes, except for Brandon. He hung back, a surly expression on his face, until everyone else had left.

"Should I say something to him?" Jessica asked Elizabeth.

"It seems only right. You two have been so *close* this week. Why don't you tell him where to get off!" Elizabeth advised.

"I just might do that," Jessica said, squaring her shoulders and heading in Brandon's direction. "Oh, Brandon!" she called softly. "Aren't you going to say goodbye? After all we've meant to each other this past week!"

Brandon's scowl deepened until his eyebrows were almost a solid black line across his forehead. He opened his mouth to speak, but then he must have changed his mind. Before Jessica reached him, he spun on one heel and marched off to his dressing room without a single word.

"What an absolute jerk!" Jessica said, turning back to Elizabeth. "Let's go home!"

"I'm with you," Elizabeth agreed, giggling. "The

least he could have done was give you a stage kiss goodbye."

Jessica giggled too and punched her sister playfully in the arm. "Oh, gosh, I'm sorry I missed *that*!"

Their sojourn as soap stars finished, the twins zipped over to the *Times*'s offices and delivered Elizabeth's third article an hour before the deadline.

"I'll bet William is pretty mad at Brandon about now," Elizabeth said as they drove home.

"Good," Jessica told her. "He deserves to be fired for what he did. How many other girls has he used to help his career along? I'm just glad I found out before it was too late to have my revenge. I wish we could have done more. I wish I could have told him what I thought of him!"

"I guess we'll just have to be satisfied that he had to do twenty-two retakes of the party scene. I'm sure Brandon had a real headache before it was over."

"It was all I could do to keep from laughing when we switched the necklace. I think that by the end, even some of the rest of the cast knew what we were doing," Jessica said.

Elizabeth giggled. "I wouldn't be surprised if William knew. No one will tell Brandon, though. They're tired of his prima-donna antics, too."

"Seriously, though, thanks, Liz," Jessica said. "I've really learned my lesson this time. My ambitions got in the way of my common sense."

"This isn't the first time," Elizabeth reminded her.

143

"I know, but it's going to be the last. Friends and true love are worth a lot more than glitter. I hope Sam will let me make this up to him."

Elizabeth pulled into their driveway. "Don't be surprised if it takes a while."

"I don't care how long it takes," Jessica declared. "I'm going to start this afternoon. Nothing, not even watching today's episode of *The Young and the Beautiful*, is going to stop me from seeing Sam!"

At that moment, the most important thing for them to do was to gather their stuff together and get to school. Elizabeth had a history test. Jessica had to pick up a stack of homework from her classes. Their parents had cleared it with the school for the girls to miss morning classes every day that week, but the makeup homework was incredible.

"I never realized how much we actually *do* in class," Jessica said, picking up the finished homework she had worked on late into the night.

"I never realized how few hours there are in a day—or how many." Elizabeth sighed. "We're doing a lot, but it still feels as if there's never enough time to get everything done."

"I know what you mean."

Just as they were walking out the door, the phone rang.

"Who could that be?" Jessica asked as she picked up the receiver. "Hello?"

She listened for a moment, then cupped her hand over the mouthpiece to talk with Elizabeth.

"It's William," she said. "Apparently the 'stud'

Brandon Hunter viewed the videotapes, and he isn't pleased with the way the final scene looks."

"No kidding!" Elizabeth remarked.

"He's threatening to quit if we don't reshoot. So William says we have to do it."

"That sounds like Brandon," Elizabeth said, quirking her eyebrow. "But when are we supposed to reshoot?"

Jessica motioned for Elizabeth to listen in on the conversation. "When are we supposed to tape it again?" she asked William. "The show airs in a couple of hours."

"We're going to have to do it live," William said. "We'll run the rest of the program, then act out the party scene before a live audience—as they say. So I want you girls to drive back to L.A. immediately."

"But, William—" Jessica began, thinking about the plans she had to spend the afternoon with Sam. She knew Elizabeth was thinking about her history test. She could see it on her face.

"There's really no choice, girls. See you soon," William said and hung up.

Jessica sighed. "No choice, he says."

"I heard him."

"This really burns me up! Brandon's scenes don't look any worse today than they do any other day."

"Well, maybe a little." Elizabeth chuckled. "I'm sure they had to leave in some of his mistakes because there just wasn't time to keep running retakes. I imagine he hates looking foolish on camera."

"That's for sure," Jessica added. "Brandon thinks he's so in control of every situation."

The girls began to gather their belongings for the trip back to L.A. While Elizabeth was calling the school to let them know what was happening, Jessica wrote a note to put on the front door for all their friends who were due to show up to watch the show, as they had all week.

This is absolutely the pits! Jessica thought to herself. *Brandon has been trying to run my life all week. He chose my clothes, he staged our publicity dates, and now he's ruining my best chance to talk to Sam before he goes away for the weekend to a bike race.*

"I'm not going to let him do this to me!" she spoke aloud. "I've just had a brainstorm. It's a perfect way to get back at Brandon once and for all and also to tell Sam that I love him and want him back in my life."

"What's going on in that devious mind of yours now?" Elizabeth asked. "And what can I do to help."

Jessica smiled. "It's going to be a surprise for Brandon. I'll tell you on the way to Los Angeles. But first, I have to call Sam."

Jessica dialed Sam's number and got his answering machine. She took a deep breath and plunged ahead. "Sam, this is Jessica. I don't have time to explain right now, but *please* watch *The Young and the Beautiful* this afternoon. It's really important. And, Sam? I love you."

Fourteen

The studio was a flurry of activity when Jessica and Elizabeth arrived later that day.

"Doing a live show. Wow! You can feel the excitement in the air," Elizabeth whispered, then winked at Jessica. "Nobody but us knows just *how* lively this show is going to be."

Jessica shivered with anticipation. "I can't wait!"

As the time drew near for the live broadcast, the actors and actresses scrambled into the same positions they had held that morning during the party scene.

"OK, the commercial is almost over. Thirty seconds, places everyone," William said. "Everybody ready? Let's make this as smooth as possible." He watched for the red light that signaled that the commercial had faded out. "And . . . action."

" 'I've been waiting for you,' " Elizabeth purred into Brandon's ear. " 'Isn't it a beautiful day? Why don't you walk with me to the window?' "

147

" 'Where's Heather?' " Brandon asked, glancing around.

" 'She'll be along,' " Elizabeth said. " 'I was hoping to speak with you alone for a moment.' "

Everything is going as it's supposed to, Jessica thought with satisfaction. *Brandon won't suspect a thing.*

Jessica entered the set from the left as she was supposed to, necklace in place and a big smile on her face.

" 'Heather!' " Brandon greeted her. " 'Tiffany and I were just talking about you. I'm so glad you were able to come.' " *He looks very sure of himself. Of course he does. He has us all jumping to do his bidding like a bunch of servants.*

"I've missed you, Jeremy," Jessica said, with just the right amount of longing in her eyes. "I hope your mother is doing well."

"Yes, she'll be discharged from the hospital tomorrow morning," Brandon said, his composure perfectly in place.

You think you're in control don't you, Brandon? Jessica thought. *Just wait!*

The scene continued as it had that morning, with Elizabeth trying to take Brandon's attention away from Jessica by declaring that she could influence the board of directors at Newtronics to donate funds to the hospital wing, then with Jessica swooning onto the sofa while Brandon ran to fetch her a glass of water.

Here it comes! Jessica had never been more ready for anything in her whole life.

" 'What was it you wanted to talk to me

about?' " Jessica cooed demurely and placed a shy, tentative hand on Brandon's arm.

Brandon scooted closer to Jessica on the sofa. He stroked her hair, just as the script dictated. " 'I want to talk about us.' "

" 'Oh.' " Jessica displayed genuine surprise. " 'I thought that you and Tiffany were an item.' "

" 'I don't care for Tiffany. I care for *you*!' " Brandon declared. He dropped off the seat and settled on one knee. " 'I love you, Heather. I've never felt like this before. Please tell me you'll be mine forever.' "

This was the point where Jessica was supposed to throw herself into Brandon's waiting arms and kiss him passionately.

Instead, she stood up and looked down on him from her superior height. " 'No, Jeremy,' " she said loudly. " 'I don't love you. The truth is, I'm in love with somebody else.' "

Brandon's mouth dropped open. "But . . ."

Jessica hurried on with her ad-lib speech while the rest of the cast at the party watched. " 'I'm in love with Sam, the boy I left behind. I could never love you the way I love him. He's caring and wonderful and kind. And you're nothing but a big jerk!' "

With a flick of her wrist, she tossed the contents of the glass of water into his face.

Jessica almost laughed when she saw the look of total shock on Brandon's face. Somehow she managed to stay in character.

"I . . . I . . . don't know what to say. . . ." Brandon sputtered. His eyes darted wildly around the stage and focused on the blinking red light over the camera.

Yes, it's on, you creep! Jessica told him silently.

Brandon's mouth opened and closed like a fish, but no sound came out. The last the viewers saw before William cut to a commercial was Brandon sinking onto the window seat with his head in his hands, and Jessica standing proud and dominant over him.

"That's a wrap, folks," William called. "Jessica, I want to speak with you."

"So do I!" Marve said angrily as he emerged from the wings, where he had witnessed the whole thing.

"Uh-oh, again!" Jessica glanced at Elizabeth, who was coming toward her, ready to lend her support.

Before William and Marve reached her, though, Brandon found his voice and exploded. "You little snot!" he yelled. "What kind of games do you think you're playing out there? No one changes my scenes without my permission! How dare you?"

"How dare *you*?" Jessica exploded back when Elizabeth had reached her side. "You've spent the last week pretending to be nice to me when you *know* that it was all an elaborate plan of yours and Marve's to garner publicity for the show! Well, your ratings might have soared *last* week, but now your fans will recognize you for the creep you really are!"

"What were you going to do, Brandon?" Elizabeth asked. "Just not call Jessica anymore? Tell the press that you dropped her?"

William glared at Marve and Brandon, neither of whom had anything to say. "I am appalled at your lack of common decency," he thundered. "Jessica and Elizabeth have done a fine job this week, and this is the way you treat them?"

"I thought it would be good for the show," Brandon said weakly.

"And you, Marve—you were in on this from the beginning?" William asked incredulously. "I am totally disgusted, and if your precious ratings drop now, it will be exactly what you deserve! Both of you!"

Jessica turned to Brandon, her eyes flashing. "I really respected you," she told him. "I watched you on the show every day and looked forward to meeting you. And then, when you asked me out, I was thrilled."

"So, we had a good time," Brandon said, trying to salvage a piece of the situation.

"Brandon Hunter, you may be a big star," Jessica said, "but you've completely forgotten how to be a human being. And I think I'll give Sandi Starr a call—to warn her about what bad news you are!"

Jessica didn't wait for a response this time. "Let's go home, Liz," she said. "We have a *life* to get back to."

The Wakefield twins exited with dignity, stage left.

"This has really been some week," Elizabeth commented as they parked at home a couple of hours later after fighting the rush-hour traffic from Los Angeles. "I'm worn out."

"Me, too."

"You haven't said much since we left the studio," Elizabeth noted. "You're really worried about the consequences of what happened today, aren't you."

"I'm worried, all right. I guess my career as an actress is over now after that stunt."

"I doubt that," Elizabeth replied. "Brandon Hunter probably doesn't have that much influence except on his own show. Anyway, even if he does, daytime TV may be out for a while, but there's always prime time!"

Jessica leaned her head against the headrest and closed her eyes. "You know, it's strange. I really don't care that much whether my career is down the tubes. I don't think I'm ready to play all the games that go with show business. They take up too much time, and they ruin your love life!"

"I know what you mean! Rodney, my editor, told me today that he's very interested in more articles from me on a regular basis, but I turned him down."

"Why? I thought free-lancing for the *Los Angeles Times* was your dream goal."

"It *was*," Elizabeth told her. "But I've realized over the past week how much time preparing and writing articles takes. I still want to write for the *Times*, but I know that I just don't have the time *right now*. I told him I'd give him a call when classes were over for the summer and I could handle a part-time job."

"I guess we both learned something this week,"

Jessica said. "There's time enough later to pursue our careers—like *after* high school, *after* college, and maybe even *after* graduate school!"

Jessica got out of the Jeep and headed up the walkway to the front door.

"We *are* only juniors in high school," Elizabeth agreed as she followed her twin. "I'm really glad that we had the opportunity to try out our careers, though."

"So you're not mad at me anymore for dragging you into this?"

Elizabeth gave her sister a big hug. "I can never stay mad at you for long, Jess."

The twins entered their house with smiles on their faces.

"Surprise!" Their parents, brother, and a big group of their friends were waiting for them.

"Congratulations, Jessica," Steven said. "You really told that jerk off!"

"Yeah, Jessica seems to be the only one around here who dares to be different," Bruce commented as he slapped her on the back.

"You two must be exhausted," Mrs. Wakefield said. "Sit down and relax. Eat!"

It was then that Elizabeth and Jessica realized that their dining-room table was laid out with food and that this was a surprise party honoring them.

"Thanks, Mom, Dad," Elizabeth said, sinking into a chair beside Todd.

Amy was still extolling Jessica's praises. Jessica couldn't even get past her to talk to Sam. "Imagine breaking up with Brandon Hunter on national TV!" she exclaimed.

Jessica nodded distractedly and looked over her friend's shoulder to where Sam was standing quietly, waiting for her to make the first move. "I wasn't ever *going* with him," Jessica said, never taking her eyes off Sam. "I lost track for a while of my true priorities. But now I know exactly what I want. Excuse me."

Jessica pushed her way through the group. When she reached Sam's side, the two of them joined hands and walked out to the relative privacy of the backyard amidst cheers from their friends.

"I meant everything I said on the show," Jessica said softly.

"And your message on the phone?" Sam asked.

"Yes, I do love you," Jessica whispered. "I hope you can forgive me for going off the deep end, *again*."

Sam didn't even hesitate. He pulled Jessica into his arms for the kiss of a lifetime. It was better than any of the stage kisses she had shared with Brandon, that was for sure!

In the middle of the kiss, Jessica dimly heard the ringing of the phone.

"Jessica!" Elizabeth called a moment later. "I'm sorry to bother you, but it's William."

Jessica groaned as she turned to go inside. "This is it," she told Sam, who came with her. "I think *I* should become a writer and write a book about how to be run out of the acting business before ever getting started."

Elizabeth smiled as Jessica walked up to her. "He said that after watching the videotape of the last scene, he's even more impressed with us than before," Elizabeth told her. "He wants to know if we're interested in negotiating a regular contract."

For a second, Jessica felt that familiar surge of excitement that always hit her when she was about to make a major decision. Then she glanced from Elizabeth's twinkling eyes to Sam's concerned expression. Just as suddenly the excitement faded and common sense took over. She looked again at Elizabeth, who was holding her hand over the phone, then at the expectant faces of her friends and family, and finally back at Sam, patiently waiting for her to make a decision.

"Tell him . . . tell him we'll think about it and get back to him," Jessica said.

As Elizabeth delivered the message and hung up, Jessica turned back to Sam and grinned. "I don't want to burn *all* my bridges."

Sam grinned back, then picked her up and swung her around. "Life around you, Jessica Wakefield, is anything but dull!"

"Look at them out there," Bruce said, jabbing a finger toward the backyard where Jessica, Sam, Elizabeth, Todd, and several others had gone after the phone call. "I thought things might get exciting around here with Jess and Liz becoming soap stars. Now it looks as though they're just going to go back to being regular high school students."

"There's nothing wrong with that," Barry remarked. "I wouldn't mind having a brief stint as a TV actor for a week—just to say I had done it."

Bruce shrugged. "I was hoping they would become big shots and start throwing parties as outrageous as the ones Jess attended in Los Angeles. At least they really know how to have a good time there," Bruce said, shaking his head. "Sweet Valley is about the most boring place on earth. We're so middle-of-the-road, it's pathetic! They could do about a one-minute TV show on this town and call it *Lifestyles of the Dull and Lifeless*."

"Oh, it's not *that* bad," Ken said. "In fact, Sweet Valley High has been chosen for some big honor. My English teacher told us in class today that a foreign delegation of some sort is coming to town to observe typical American high school life."

"I heard about that, too. It's a delegation of teachers, I think, because the coach was talking about showing around a fellow coach from Germany," Terri said, coming up and looping her arms around Ken's shoulders.

"It's just the same dull, boring routine that happens every time some big shot shows up in Sweet Valley." Bruce frowned—and then he got a nasty gleam in his eye. "Maybe I should shake things up a bit."

What does Bruce have in mind?
Find out in Sweet Valley High #86,
JESSICA AGAINST BRUCE.